I turned and began to walk along the upper side of the beach, passing in and out of the black serrated shadows of the palm leaves. Lee paced with me, silent.

We might have been alone on a deserted island: the noise from the bar had faded, to be replaced by the ripple of water running gently up the sand and the faint rustle of leaves as the warm perfumed air moved gently under the silver light.

As we stood facing each other I was silent, mesmerized by the moonlight, by the soft air, by her physical proximity. She took my hand. The contact was enough to compel me to take that one step into her arms.

I could smell her light perfume, feel the taut muscles in her back, hear a murmur deep in her throat. We kissed gently, carefully ... But then Lee's mouth opened beneath mine, her tongue flickered along my lips, her arms tightened about me.

I wanted to draw back. Lee was making demands I couldn't, wouldn't meet. I heard myself groan ...

ABOUT THE AUTHOR

CLAIRE McNAB is the author of twelve Detective
Inspector Carol Ashton mysteries: *Lessons in Murder,
Fatal Reunion, Death Down Under, Cop Out, Dead
Certain, Body Guard, Double Bluff, Inner Circle,
Chain Letter, Past Due, Set Up,* and *Under Suspicion.*
The thirteenth, *Death Club,* is due out in May, 2001.
She has written two romances, *Under the Southern
Cross* and *Silent Heart,* and has co-authored a
self-help book, *The Loving Lesbian,* with Sharon
Gedan. She is the author of two Denise Cleever
thrillers, *Murder Undercover* and *Death Understood.*
The third in the series, *Out of Sight,* comes out in
October, 2001.

In her native Australia Claire is known for her
crime fiction, plays, children's novels and self-help
books.

Now permanently resident in Los Angeles, she
teaches fiction writing in the UCLA Extension
Writers' Program. She makes it a point to return to
Australia once a year to refresh her Aussie accent.

Under the Southern Cross

BY CLAIRE MCNAB

THE NAIAD PRESS, INC.
2001

Printed in the United States of America on acid-free paper
First Edition
First Printing April, 1992
Second Printing September, 1992
Third Printing April, 1994
Fourth Printing February, 1997
Fifth Printing February 2001

Edited by Katherine V. Forrest
Cover design by Pat Tong and Bonnie Liss
   (Phoenix Graphics)
Typeset by Sandi Stancil

Library of Congress Cataloging-in-Publication Data

McNab, Claire.
   Under the Southern Cross / Claire McNab.
      p.   cm.
   ISBN 1-56280-011-6
   I. Title.
PS3563.C3877U5   1992
813ê.54—dc20

91-36565
CIP

For Gwyn and Cath
(AKA Trish and Suzie)

ACKNOWLEDGMENTS

TO MY EDITOR IN AUSSIE-SPEAK:

Fair dinkum, a writer'd have Buckley's of finding another bonzer editor like Katherine V. Forrest — bewdy bottler!

SPECIAL THANKS TO:

Lyn and Glenda, aficionados of Queensland.

Barbara, tourism guru.

CHAPTER ONE

I love flying, especially in small planes, where the experience gives me a little of the exhilaration birds must feel when they ride the wind.

This time I was sitting just behind the pilot in a little twenty-seater, leaning forward to see the green wrinkled water crawling by beneath us.

He grinned at me over his shoulder, raising his voice above the insect drone of the engines. "Paradise, eh, Alex?"

I smiled acknowledgment and he turned back to his instruments. He was right — it was paradise.

Below us scattered islands lazed in the warm tropical sea by the flank of Queensland. From this height vegetation looked like verdant stubble and the water was so clear that I could see, as if on a gigantic contour map, the tones of green, aquamarine and blue that showed the gradations of depth. As our little plane advanced slowly over the shallow sea, its shadow flickering and dancing, each new island showed its unique underwater pattern of banks and channels, shaded here and there with darker patches of seaweed.

I knew that to the east, where the cold blue of the Pacific Ocean broke its might against the coral walls of the Great Barrier Reef, the continental shelf suddenly plunged to icy black depths. But here everything was drenched in light and the water was tamed, soothed by the warmth, lapping indolently against white coral beaches.

The pilot raised his voice so that the passengers crammed into the cabin could hear: "Tern Island ahead."

It was almost a routine destination for me now, but the impact of its beauty had hardly been dulled by familiarity.

Two thirds of the island formed a national park protected from development, so the hills and valleys were blanketed with a heavy coating of virgin rainforest and at the sea's edge mangrove swamps met the salty water. Tern Island Resort began where the thick natural cover met the manicured precision of a nine-hole golf course. From the air most of the buildings clustered around the pale crescent of Tern Beach were almost hidden by the luxuriance of tropical gardens.

We went into a shallow dive, swooping low over a couple of bright-sailed windsurfers scudding in zig-zag patterns across the turquoise water. As usual, the single tarmac strip of the airport looked far too small to me, but as we approached it seemed to stretch until it was a respectable length. I know that landings are the most dangerous part of air travel, so I always hold my breath in those last moments before touchdown. This time the wheels struck the gray-black surface with a pounding whoomp, then, shuddering, we scooted down the strip. The pilot was smiling: I wondered if he'd deliberately come in a little fast.

We made a wide circle and taxied back to the little terminal building, which was situated halfway down the strip. The door was opened, the steps extended the short distance to the ground, and a babble of different accents broke out as passengers extricated themselves from the cramped cabin and stretched in the moist, heavy warmth.

They were all seasoned travelers, so I didn't follow them immediately, taking time to pin my identification to my white shirt. I've always hated being labeled, but Sir Frederick had insisted that during a convention, staff wear their names at all times. The badge was a large rectangle, conspicuous with Australia's national colors of green and gold. The symbol for Australasian Pan Pacific is an elaborate representation of the initials within an outline of Australia. I checked to make sure the name ALEXANDRA FINDLAY was straight.

Confirming that my shirt was tucked neatly into my tailored white pants — "Appearance is eighty percent of success!" according to Sir Frederick — I

3

joined the gaggle of passengers. As I shepherded them towards the diminutive blossom-and-creeper-covered building that served as Tern Island's airport terminal, I saw that Steve Monahan was part of the welcoming committee waiting with glasses of champagne and orange.

"G'day," Steve was saying cheerfully to each person as he handed out refreshments. As always, I was cynically amused at the up-market ultra-Australian impression he had created for himself. Tall, fair-haired, tanned, and with an engaging grin, he wore tight beige shorts with a thin snakeskin belt, a matching shirt with several superfluous pockets, and a sand-colored Akubra hat with a bright feather in the band and one side turned up in the approved fashion.

I was put on my guard when he smiled at me with special warmth. "Hi, Alex. Mind if I ask you a favor?"

Working with him had taught me that his friendliness concealed a strong self-interest and an unremittingly manipulative nature. I said shortly, "What?"

His amusement deepened at my lack of enthusiasm. "It's not much to ask, love," he said persuasively. "Just that there's a few more VIPs flying in this afternoon about three and I can't be here to meet the plane. Would you do it for me?"

"All right, but you owe me one, Steve."

I lost his attention as his glance shifted to Hilary Ferguson, the representative for one of the British tour wholesalers. It's not often that someone lives up to the description of ravishingly beautiful, but Hilary Ferguson did. Petite, with cornflower blue eyes and fresh, high skin color, she had masses of chestnut hair, a wide, white smile, and, in a fetching final touch, dimples. She spoke in the half-swallowed vowels that implied membership in the British elite, but in my short acquaintance with her I'd found her friendly and unpretentious.

Steve gave his best larrikin grin. "Well, g'day!"

I left him trying to impress Hilary with as many Aussie cliches as he could cram into his conversation, and began to apportion the guests to their respective mini-buses.

I'd just checked that everyone in my bus had their cabin luggage from the plane when Steve put his head through the door. "I forgot to tell you, Alex, that your special responsibility will be on that flight. It'll impress Sir Frederick no end if you go out of your way to meet the woman."

I stepped out of the bus so we wouldn't be overheard. "Pity that discretion isn't one of your major qualities, Steve."

He ignored my criticism, saying with a tinge of malice, "You're going to have your work cut out — Lee Paynter won't be easy to please."

"You know, Steve, sometimes I wonder how I got along before I had you to advise me."

"Just being friendly, Alex," he said, amused. "The woman's pretty formidable, you know."

"Makes me all the more surprised that you're giving up the opportunity to meet Lee Paynter yourself. Would have thought you'd want to make an immediate impression on someone so influential."

"We've met before, love, in the States, and I found her impervious to my charms."

"Surely not!"

5

He grinned at my mockery. "Well, darl, I'm good, but not *that* good. Wouldn't have a chance. Apart from the fact she's married to her business, she's also a lesbian." He gave the word a strong emphasis, pausing for a moment before he added, "And she's upfront about it, too." His smile widened as he said teasingly, "*You* could always give it a go, Alex. Try a walk on the wild side for a change. You never know, she might just have a weakness for the dark sultry sort."

I matched his flippant tone. "Whatever you may think, there's a limit to what I'll do for my career."

He raised a scornful eyebrow. "There's a limit to what you'd do for anything or anyone, love. I mean, you turned *me* down flat. You just don't like to get involved, do you?"

"Try not to take it so much to heart," I said, smiling to take the bite from my words.

Steve narrowed his eyes. "If I were you, I'd be careful. For instance, I'd certainly think twice before I turned Sir Frederick down ..."

He gave me no chance for a caustic reply, leaping up into his bus with a cheerful, "Let her rip!" to the driver.

The little electric buses zipped along the narrow roadways, each taking its load of passengers and luggage to the appropriate section of the resort. I was on automatic, answering questions and responding politely when appreciative comments were made at the rich beauty of the vegetation whipping past the windows. Before the first passenger got out I gave a brief outline of the program for the rest of the day and the details of the seafood banquet in

6

the evening which would be hosted by Sir Frederick Salway, Pan Pacific's managing director.

It took an hour for me and the attentive Tern Island staff to settle each representative into his or her accommodation, and I was heartily tired of smiling when I finally stood alone on the veranda of my own little cabana.

Apart from the administration and entertainment center, most of the buildings on Tern Island were artfully concealed behind screens of exuberant tropical greenery. There were three grades of residences: two-story blocks of self-contained family units; luxurious cabins, each with a private garden; small cabanas — suitable for one or two — nestling in the coconut palms fringing the crescent of the beach.

The lazy heat of the island matched my own sudden uncharacteristic lethargy. I yawned as an imperious peacock spread his spectacular tail feathers for my inspection. "You're very handsome," I said. He eyed me with disdain before strutting off to examine an opulent bush. A breeze trifled with the heavy fronds of the palms arching above me, gaudy butterflies fluttered among the extravagant blooms — what more could I want from life than to be part of this beauty?

After checking that I had enough free time before my luncheon duties, I changed into a swimming costume, applied liberal amounts of sunscreen — even though I have olive skin and tan easily — and walked the short distance from my cabana to the bleached coral sand. Its fine grains squeaked under my bare feet and small crabs skittered sideways as my shadow fell across them. There was no surf — the Great Barrier Reef prevented the advance of the dark blue Pacific rollers, so here the pastel water lapped gently. I waded into the clear tepid liquid, enjoying its sensuous touch, and, when it was deep enough to swim, a few desultory strokes took me out from the beach. Turning on my back, I squinted through the dazzling glare.

It was a scene worthy of a glossy brochure. The white beach with strategically placed recliners and a sprinkling of sun-worshippers, a backdrop of coconut palms, and underneath their shade the rich colors of hibiscus blossoms set against the luscious green of fleshy plants and ferns. In contrast, the mangroves crowding into the water at the southern end of the beach were a darker, danker shade and, with their miniature forests of breathing roots thrusting up through the sand, somewhat sinister.

I didn't want to leave the caress of the languid water, but I had a schedule of duties for the afternoon. I swam slowly back to shore, collected my towel and dark glasses, checked the time, and retreated for a few more minutes to the scanty shade provided by the fronds overhanging the upper edge of the beach.

As I reclined on the sand my thoughts shifted to Lee Paynter. For the past twelve months I'd been concentrating on tapping the potential of the European tourism market, but even so I was aware of the American's name and reputation.

In the world travel market, Lee Paynter had been described as the archetypal American business operator, a spectacularly successful entrepreneur who had introduced her conducted tours to previously unreceptive countries, wheeling and dealing her way through the labyrinths of officialdom. It was rumored that she would bribe, blackmail, or use any of her contacts in the U.S. government if her considerable personal charm failed to achieve what she wanted.

I picked up a handful of the fine coral sand and let it filter between my fingers. The involvement of Lee Paynter's company in the Pacific region would undoubtedly be advantageous to tourism, so Australasian Pan Pacific, the private industry body set up by Australian and New Zealand travel interests, had actively courted her interest. I knew it was a considerable coup to have a tour wholesaler with Lee Paynter's clout involved in the convention, and an even more considerable achievement to have her agree to personally assess both the destinations and the Australian ground operators.

In Sydney at the briefing before the convention, Sir Frederick Salway, head of A.P.P., had said to me with his charismatic smile, "Alexandra, I want you to regard Lee Paynter as your special responsibility. You'll be her minder, and I want you to keep her happy. Do whatever she asks ..." Under his neat white mustache his mouth had twitched as he added, "... within reason, of course."

Now I wondered if there had been a double meaning there — if he'd assumed I'd know that Lee Paynter was gay.

"And Alexandra," he had concluded, "we're giving you this opportunity to show us what you're made of. Pull it off, and your career gets a boost — I can guarantee that."

I loved my work — I'd been hooked on the industry ever since my first job in a travel agency —

and now there was a real chance that A.P.P. would be creating an expanded network to encourage more Asians to visit Australia. With my European experience I'd have a good chance of being on the short list for area management.

Sir Frederick recognized my ambition and was simply giving me a range of opportunities to demonstrate my abilities. There was nothing personal in his attention, so I could safely ignore Steve's snide remark ... or could I? Lately I'd had the niggling feeling that there might be more to Sir Frederick's attention than professional interest.

Hunger made me aware that I should be dressing for lunch. I stood, stretched, took one last regretful look at the curving beach, and walked the few steps to my cabana.

My thoughts returned to Lee Paynter. I had the strong conviction that dealing with her would present me with what management seminars euphemistically call "a challenge." And I had to pull it off — no matter how difficult the woman could be. I felt as though I were about to engage in battle with a dangerous opponent. What armor could I use? And the answer was immediate: indifference, well-disguised with courtesy, was my best defense.

That afternoon, instead of riding back to the airport in a mini-bus, I decided to give myself time to walk the distance at a leisurely pace. As I strolled along the well-kept paths I admired the skillful way the resort was landscaped, so that the rich tropical growth seemed to naturally dispose itself to advantage, disguising buildings and lining the winding paths with color and lavish greenery.

A short, sturdy pier marked the end of the beach, and I paused to admire the yachts swinging at anchor. Beside the heavy wooden piles a white egret slowly waded, its attention fixed on the rippling water. Then with one swift thrust it extended its long neck to seize some marine tidbit. A rapid swallow, and it resumed its remorseless concentration. Amusing myself by imagining life from the perspective of a small crustacean, I decided that oblivion in the form of an egret snack would at least be quick.

I walked along the pier, my sandaled feet echoing hollowly on the worn wooden planks. A solitary black and white pelican eyed me dourly, its pouched beak sunk into its downy chest. I leaned against the railing and considered the yachts. The sunlight burnished the heaving water and the white vessels seemed to be testing their tethers as though anxious to be gone. I found myself smiling at them. One day, I promised myself, I'd sail the Queensland coast, enjoy the beauties of the Whitsunday Passage, stop at deserted islands at dusk, fish for dinner, lie on the deck and watch the Milky Way revolve overhead . . .

But I couldn't do that alone — such an experience had to be shared.

Suddenly somber, I thought, Then I'll never do it.

I'd wasted time. Unless I hurried, I'd be late for the flight. The warm air, earlier a pleasure, now seemed a thick impediment to my progress. I swore at myself: first impressions are vital, and I wanted Lee Paynter to see me as cool, disciplined and efficient, not out of breath and sweating.

CHAPTER TWO

The plane wasn't on schedule, no doubt keeping what's derisively called "Queensland time," so I could catch my breath and chat idly with others in the welcoming committee before the flight arrived.

"Hi, Alex. Want a hibiscus behind your ear?" Tony Englert, a cheerful, chubby extrovert, was Sir Frederick's second in command. "It'll give you a sort of raffish, laid-back air. Just the thing to impress your Yank."

As I laughingly declined we heard the buzz of the approaching plane. In the distance it looked like

13

an elaborate radio-controlled toy. It roared across the bay with noisy purpose, landed smoothly and taxied promptly to halt in front of the warm peach tints of the *Welcome to Tern Island* sign. I stood back, conscious that I felt a slight anxiety ... perhaps wariness would be a better word.

First onto the tarmac was a woman immediately recognizable from press photographs I'd seen. Lee Paynter wore a severely cut pale blue summer-weight suit. Silver jewelry flashed in the glaring sunlight as she walked briskly towards us, briefcase in hand, assurance in every step. Moving forward to greet her, I saw she was of medium height, although she seemed taller because she carried her chin confidently high and held her shoulders back. Her short, well-styled hair was blonde, but streaked with a few tawny shades. The lines of her face were definite: a slightly hooked nose, firm mouth and strong jawline. When she took her dark glasses off, I found myself assessed by direct, slate gray eyes.

I smiled, shook her hand. I thought, What are you seeing, other than a woman who is a little taller, a little heavier than you, with dark hair and eyes, and a carefully welcoming expression? Or am I simply someone in the background to smooth your way, and not worth a second look?

Lee Paynter glanced at my identification. "Do you go by Alexandra?"

"Alex will do."

"Okay. And I'm Lee, of course."

She had what I call a light American accent, a lilt that catches familiar words and gives them an unfamiliar spin. And blonde though she was, her

14

voice had a dark quality, a low timbre that stopped just short of huskiness.

The pleasantries disposed of, Lee Paynter turned her attention to business. She looked past me at the staff engaged with the new arrivals. "I want to check the entry procedures here. What I'm looking for is unobtrusive, efficient service that can process a tour group quickly, get them settled in, ready to enjoy themselves." Her focus returning to me, she added, "And then I'd like to unwind with a game of tennis. Can you match me with someone who can play?"

"I'll give you a game."

"Can you play well?"

Nettled, I said sharply, "Yes, I can."

My vehemence earned me a slight smile from the American, but no comment. As we walked towards the mini-buses I began to outline the resort's guest registration procedures, careful not to let my voice show the irritation this peremptory woman had caused in me.

My shoulders were tight. Already I sensed that indifference was an option I no longer had.

The brassy heat of the late afternoon had discouraged other players, so we had the courts to ourselves. Choosing one sheltered from the sunlight by a tall cluster of palms, we began to hit up.

I felt apprehensive. She was an unknown quantity. Well-described by others, but still an enigma to me. I knew the general details, the steady advance of her business, her reputation for tough negotiation, but that was no more than rough guidance in working out how to manage her, given the nuances of interpersonal relationships.

Lee's tight white shorts and brief top revealed a well-cared body, lightly tanned, full-breasted and athletic. She had obviously been taught classic tennis: she moved quickly to prepare for each shot and she hit each ball cleanly.

I watched her narrowly. The casual arrogance of her "Can you play well?" had stung and I didn't want her to underestimate me. Soon I was caught up in the familiar rhythmic pleasure of tennis — the joy of changing direction smoothly, balancing, striking. At the other end Lee mirrored my efforts, fluidly stroking the ball.

A hit-up with an unfamiliar opponent is for testing skills, probing for weaknesses, assessing strengths. I can usually force myself to be patient, but anxiety made me say, too soon, "Shall we start?"

Lee smiled briefly. "I have a feeling I may have met my match."

She played with the resolution I expected, taking every opportunity to press an advantage, disguising her own limitations and evaluating my game for shortcomings that could be exploited. This was no relaxed, social match — each of us intended to win.

And, at least in tennis, I'm accustomed to winning. I play A-Grade and have a kicking serve, reliable ground-strokes and a bustling net-game. Perhaps more importantly, from the time I was a child playing competition tennis my parents had drilled into me *Never give up*, so I'll fight back, even when a match seems irretrievably lost.

I analyzed Lee Paynter as each game went with

service, realizing that technically at least, I was the superior player, although I had an opponent who showed a tenacity that meant no point could be guaranteed, no matter how bullet-like the delivery or careful the placement. Lee covered the court with deceptive ease, hit the ball hard and squarely, and refused to be intimidated by the speed and accuracy of my best shots.

It took all my concentration to win the first set, breaking Lee's service to take it six-four. I made the mistake of relaxing a little, and when the second set began with a relentless attack from Lee, within a few minutes I found myself down two games. The battle exhilarated, stimulated me. Focused, I clawed my way back to even the score at two-all.

I considered, Let her have this set? She might take it anyway, and my job's to make things easy for her — not irritate her by winning.

Lee took advantage of my lapse in concentration to win the next two games. Down two-four, I grinned to myself: To hell with it! I'll beat her if I can.

By now we were both breathless, wet with perspiration and taut with purpose. Pushing my game up a notch, I belted the ball with all my strength and skill. Lee responded with stubborn intent. She tried to reach everything — even shots that seemed clear winners — used cunning lobs to vary the pace, hammered at the slight weakness I've got on my forehand side, and generally tried to run me off my feet.

At six-all, Lee gasped, "Play advantage? It's more tennis than a tie-break."

Although I was beginning to wilt in the sticky heat, I agreed immediately. The thwack as racket hit ball, the pattern of anticipation, movement, preparation, stroke — hypnotized me. My opponent became a partner in a ritual that was more than just a tennis match ... it was a contest where mind and body combined for defined rewards, where the ambiguities of social interaction were replaced by the certainties of rules and conventions. It was almost with disappointment that I hit the last winning shot down the sideline.

Lee laughed as she ceremoniously shook my hand. "That was great. I can't remember when I enjoyed being beaten. I *would* like a chance to get even, though. How about early tomorrow morning before it gets too hot? Can we fit another match into the program?"

"Do you want to skip the horse-riding? That's on your schedule before breakfast. And then there's a visit to the artists' colony."

"I'll stick to the schedule. I always like to check out everything myself. I'll take a rain check on the tennis." She looked at me speculatively. "Do you ride as well as you play tennis?"

"Not quite." I had responded rather more sharply than I'd intended because I felt that Lee Paynter, accustomed to valuing people purely on their use to her, was deciding whether, apart from my skills at tennis, I was worthy of further attention.

"Buy you a drink?" said Lee, apparently oblivious to my challenging tone.

Perversely, I didn't want my vexation dulled by her hospitality, and her friendly tone made me wary. I checked my watch, shook my head, said with requisite regret, "I hadn't realized how long our match took. Sorry, I've still got some things to do before tonight's presentation dinner ... Would you like me to arrange for refreshments to be sent to your cabana, or would you prefer a drink by the poolside?"

"I can look after myself, thanks. See you this evening."

Effectively dismissed, I watched her stride away, purposeful, and, to me, aggravatingly arrogant. To be fair, I had to admit that Lee Paynter had every reason to be self-assured — she had earned the prestige and influence she'd attained.

I've always been adept at hiding my feelings, so I knew it was unlikely she had recognized the uncertainty I felt. I wanted her to see me as cool, controlled, confident, so she could not guess the importance of her satisfaction to my career.

From the official table, I surveyed the room. A hum of anticipation was filling the dining hall as guests found their seats. Outside, the warm darkness of the tropical night had fallen with its usual abruptness. Inside, illuminated by almost hectic brightness, the seafood was elaborately displayed — a smorgasbord on tables decorated with exotic ferns and extravagant blossoms. Huge overflowing plates of oysters, prawns, lobsters, Morton Bay bugs, crayfish, gigantic crabs and goggle-eyed fish jostled for space with a selection of intriguing salads and fat loaves of bread.

I had arrived early with Tony Englert, Sir Frederick's assistant, to ensure things would go smoothly. Our duties completed, Tony went off to snaffle a bottle of wine, our reward, he said, for conspicuous accomplishment. He came back with a fine chardonnay, filled both our glasses, and launched into a scurrilously amusing account about a bumbling government official's interference in private tourism. He finished his story with a shout of laughter, then squeezed my hand as he pantomimed a suggestive leer. "Alex, my darling, you look absolutely ravishing in blue."

"And you," I rejoined, "look totally irresistible in off-white." I considered his pale suit. "Perhaps more off, than white."

Tony is one of the few people with whom I can immediately relax. Although nice is a bland word, nice is what he is — nice to know and nice to be with. He's clever, but his manner is open and uncomplicated, and his generosity of spirit matches his expansive body.

He leaned back in his chair, which creaked a protest. "So, how's La Paynter?"

"We had a game of tennis this afternoon ... and I'm afraid I beat her."

"Oh, bad career move!"

I laughed at his lugubrious expression. "You think I've blown it?"

"Probably not. Lee likes it straight down the line. And if she admires you, you've got it made."

"Do you know her well, Tony?"

"No better than anyone else, but one thing I can say is I think you're the right one to handle her." He grinned at my questioning expression. "Because, Alex darling, you'll be a challenge — and Lee Paynter loves a challenge."

"Meaning?"

But he refused to elaborate. Looking at his watch, he announced he had to wait for Sir Frederick at the entrance to the dining hall. I chatted idly with others at the official table, including Steve Monahan, who had obviously wasted no time in striking up a friendship with the beautiful Hilary Ferguson. He'd made an ostentatious show of gallantry when he'd escorted her to her chair, and was now assuring us of the positive impression he had made. I tuned out his familiar boasts, sipping my wine as I surveyed each table, automatically ticking off names as I recognized faces. The successful operators in international tourism belonged to a profitable world-wide club, and many of the guests knew each other through business contracts, so the hum of conversation was frequently punctuated by bursts of laughter and enthusiastic greetings.

In situations like this, listening to the easy banter, to the skill of casual, light conversation, always made me conscious of my apartness, my detachment. And, as usual, I asked myself why. It wasn't that I failed to respond to people, to feel affection for them, to become involved in their lives — but rather that I had an innate caution that prevented me from allowing indulgence in too much emotion. I had to be in control.

Control: it was a word I often used. I felt secure when I was in command — when I could be sure there'd be little chance of unwelcome surprises.

I thought sardonically, Let's not be too critical here ... I can be spontaneous too — just so long as I've planned for it.

Sometimes I wondered if there might be a

dimension missing in me, a level of deeper feeling that most other people seemed to experience. I'd never been quite sure what my friends meant when they said they were in love. The wrenching, passionate feelings they described seemed to me rather closer to discomfort than ecstasy.

Still, I could reassure myself that I was capable of the emotion itself. I loved a few close friends, and I certainly loved my parents. Sure, they'd been strict and undemonstrative in my childhood, but I'd never doubted their love for me.

In my early twenties I'd been upset when they'd decided to move out of Sydney to Canberra, where my mother's only sister lives with her family. Of course, the decision to move had been my mother's. She's soft-spoken, never loses her temper, nor, indeed, shows any strong feelings — but she always gets her own way. Now, I see my family infrequently. We have never made a fuss of birthdays or Christmas, but I always try to get down to Canberra for my parents' birthdays, which are both in June, and again in December for a family Christmas.

December made me think of Carl's birthday, and then, unwillingly, of my marriage. Now, years after the divorce, I still couldn't imagine why I'd married Carl, why I'd believed that a few words in a church would magically transform me from a reserved young woman into a warm and loving wife.

Memories I usually ignored came crowding in. I hadn't been a virgin, hadn't gone ignorant to my marriage bed. On the contrary, I'd set out to gain sexual experience deliberately, following the example of my peer group, but always, it seemed to me now, puzzled at their excited enthusiasm for an act I found not unpleasant, but essentially meaningless.

I'd been very fond of Carl and enjoyed his company. We grew up together, had many interests in common and came from similar backgrounds, so the thought of being with him permanently hadn't seemed threatening or impossible. It had been pleasant to be comfortably part of the dating game, to have by my side a tall, presentable male. Still, I was cautious, and wanted to live with him before taking the final step, but my parents' strict standards eliminated this as an option. And Carl seemed so *sure,* so convinced that we belonged together.

As part of the conventional majority, I could put to one side the disquieting attraction I felt towards my own sex ... feelings I persuaded myself would fade in time — desires that were forbidden, unthinkable. With Carl it was girlfriend and boyfriend — a safe, ordinary relationship with the obligatory sex when opportunities could be found. And I could still escape Carl's sometimes suffocating closeness and go home to my own room, my own bed. Even then my dreams, my outrageous fantasies betrayed me — they were full of luscious women to whom I turned with guilty delight.

Somehow I'd convinced myself that these yearnings would evaporate in the reality of constant heterosexuality.

I'd thought myself well prepared, but the enforced intimacy of marriage was an assault upon my private self. It wasn't Carl's fault — he was kind, affectionate, and I in turn did my best to play the role expected of me. And on the surface I succeeded, because no one seemed to sense that anything was wrong. My parents were approving; Carl began to talk of starting a family.

He said he loved me; he certainly desired me. Looking back over the years I find it strange that I can hardly picture his face, but can so clearly remember his exultation at his possession of me, his hands always greedy for my body.

Vivid too, as though preserved on film, is that one decisive night. At first, it seemed like any other evening. Carl, exhausted with lovemaking, was asleep, one arm curled around me, that unconscious embrace the posture of a proprietor. I lay looking at the patterns thrown by streetlights onto the ceiling and said into the darkness, "That's it. No more."

Why that particular night? Perhaps it had been Carl's considerate tyranny, as, anxious for my sexual response to match his, he had said almost plaintively, "Darling, it's no good for me unless you come too." Faking it was so much easier than straining for an orgasm that lovemaking almost never achieved, but this time I rebelled against the imperative to perform on schedule, trying to make a joke of my failure — "I must be tired and have a headache" — but Carl was assiduous in his pursuit of my pleasure. At last, driven to feign a climax, I fulfilled his requirements.

Lying there, quiet beside his sleeping contentment, I felt a flood of relief at my decision, even though I knew it would mean facing my parents' incomprehension and Carl's bewilderment and anguish. I realized that it would be almost impossible to explain, so I was prepared, almost eager, to be blamed, because it would help to lessen the guilt.

Indeed, Carl had been distraught, my parents astonished. "Divorce?" my mother had said as though the word itself had an unpleasant taste. "Surely not, Alex. A short separation perhaps, but not a final thing like that."

But it had been the final thing like that. Carl had resisted to the final decree, then, baffled, he had at last left me alone.

I withdrew from my memories as Sir Frederick arrived. He paused for a moment at the entrance to survey the dining room. Tall, impeccably dressed in a light summer suit, his tanned skin in contrast to his thick white hair, his imposingly aristocratic nose set off by the neat lines of his white mustache, he strode through the room, smiling and nodding as his glance fell upon a particularly important guest. I watched his progress with amused respect, knowing that it was carefully rehearsed. Late that afternoon we'd gone through the seating plan together, ensuring that the most influential tourist luminaries would receive special attention.

The hum of conversation stopped and he began his short, humorous, yet trenchant welcoming speech, his British accent only slightly blunted by years in Australia. I admired his effortless skill in holding the attention of the hundred or so hardened professionals who made up his audience.

I'd noticed Lee Paynter come in just after Sir Frederick and take her seat a little to the side of the main table. She wore a simple white linen dress, her only jewelry a fine mesh silver bracelet that shimmered as she raised her glass. She appeared to be listening attentively to Sir Frederick, her slate gray eyes fixed on him, her mouth curling into a smile at the appropriate times. Then suddenly she turned her head to look directly at me.

I felt ridiculously exposed, as though caught doing something wrong. I acknowledged our eye contact with a polite smile, then glanced away, putting on a pretense of close attention to Sir Frederick's speech.

There was no reason for the alarm that shrilled in me. Lee Paynter couldn't know that we were linked by our fundamental natures, or that I felt an insidious tug of attraction towards her. And she would never know. My career, my relationship with my parents — both had nearly been destroyed before, and there was no way I'd risk that happening again.

Be rational, Alex. You're going to be associated with Lee Paynter for a couple of weeks. So what's she to you? Just someone to manage, whose satisfaction at the service provided will reflect well on you.

It was a fair transaction — I would use Lee Paynter as Lee Paynter would use me — a useful person in the context of the situation.

Sir Frederick concluded with a graceful turn of phrase, there was applause, and the focus of attention became the spectacular seafood display.

Although fond of shellfish, I find the voracious hands-on approach off-putting. Plates piled to overflowing, the diners plunged wholeheartedly into cracking carapaces, gouging out white fish, sucking noisily at crustacean legs, gulping oysters — all of this accomplished with a full-mouthed enthusiasm more conventional meals never seemed to engender.

As soon as it was politic to do so, I escaped to walk alone along the deserted beach. The moon had not yet risen and the stars shone brilliantly. As always, I located the constellation of the Southern Cross. Seen only in the southern hemisphere, its configuration part of the Australian flag, to me it is also a personal talisman, its beauty and constancy a reassurance in a capricious world.

I stood with my hands behind my back and stared upward at the five stars and two bright pointers.

I'm happier alone ...

I frowned, wondering why I'd needed to remind myself of this at all.

CHAPTER THREE

Lee was dressed in a crisp white shirt, tailored jodhpurs and boots when I came to collect her in the cool of the early morning. Immediately I felt at a disadvantage. Having no formal riding gear, I was wearing ancient jeans. No doubt this bloody woman had the perfect outfit for every occasion.

I said, "No riding crop?"

Lee smiled at the hint of mockery. "I left the hunting jacket and hat at home, too."

It had rained during the night, and the washed air was like wine. We rode up to the stables in a little electric buggy and as we traveled along the edge of the golf course I saw her glancing appreciatively at a striking red-haired woman teeing off with a companion for an early morning game.

Surprised at my thoughts, I looked away. *Don't you care that people know you're gay ... that they say things behind your back?* Then, more resentfully, *Are you after some action? If so, you can find it on your own.*

Lee said, "Do you play golf?"

The red-haired woman had completed a graceful swing at the ball. I said, "That's Sharon Castell. She's our publicity officer and a very good golfer — much better than I am. I'll arrange a game with her, if you like." I was almost tempted to add that Sharon was very much married to a professional football player.

"I met Sharon in the States — she was part of the A.P.P. team. And yes, I'd enjoy a game of golf with her."

"I'll see what I can do."

At the stables a small group of early-risers were uneasily eying a bunch of bored horses. A whippet-thin man, tightening girths and checking bridles, said to us in a flat nasal voice, "You two ridden before?" He grunted at our affirmations. "We'll see."

Gesturing at two horses tethered apart from the others, he said, "Mind, you'd better be dinkum, because if you're not, those two will sort you out."

He watched critically as Lee adjusted the stirrups, then mounted the gray with confident grace. When I swung myself up into the saddle of the big restless bay, he grunted again. "Okay, you'll do. Might as well go ahead while I nursemaid this lot over here. The trail's signposted down to the beach. When you get there, ride along to the end of it, and wait. And don't do anything stupid. Right?"

The trail wound through the rainforest, a red-earth gouge in the brilliant greens of the tropical undergrowth. Luxuriant ferns, prized items in cooler climates, grew in wild profusion underneath the thick foliage of trees and creepers. There was a warm, moist, heavy smell of rotting wood and humus — not unpleasant, but pervasive.

We walked the horses, then trotted, finally cantering as the trail flattened out into a wider swathe through the crowding vegetation. I hadn't been on a horse for a long time, but my body remembered the balance and rhythm that made riding so enjoyable and I smiled at the scent of horse and leather. Glancing at Lee Paynter, I was unsurprised to find that she rode with a relaxed, confident style that suggested considerable riding experience.

I had to smile at my chagrin. Did she do every bloody thing well?

We came out onto the beach on the opposite side of the island, a long narrow strip of ocher sand edged on one side by small foaming waves whipped up by a stiff breeze, and on the other by a tangle of vegetation and debris washed up in storms. Out from the shore several sailboard riders skimmed their bright craft before the wind in a precarious balance between optimum speed or an ignominious dunking. Otherwise we were alone.

Lee's gray horse lifted his feet high, dancing with impatience against the tight rein. Lee looked across at my bay gelding, similarly restless. "Race you!" she challenged.

"You're on!"

Released, the horses were joyously away, their hoofs rhythmically pounding the hard-packed sand. I'd driven my heels into the bay's flanks and he'd leaped like a thoroughbred into the gallop, leaving the gray behind. I leaned over his neck, urging him to greater speed. His mane whipped back in my face, the trees and bushes on my left blurred into a continuous green wall, a flock of seagulls rose in noisy protest.

Lee had set the gray on the hard sand at the edge of the water, and his pounding feet threw sheets of drenching spray as he gained on the bay.

"Got you!" she shouted as she drew level.

I stood in the stirrups as my horse gathered himself to jump a huge fallen tree that blocked the beach. Alive with fear and excitement, I shouted as he landed cleanly and resumed his headlong gallop.

Looking back over my shoulder, I saw that Lee had skirted the dead branches by riding further out into the water, and was again closing the distance between us. She was a superb rider, perfectly balanced and daring, and she swept past me just before the beach ended in a tangle of driftwood.

She skidded to a graceful stop in a shower of sand — I narrowly missed falling as my horse abruptly straightened his legs to accomplish a similar sudden halt.

"One each," said Lee. "You win at tennis, I win at horse-racing."

Sitting easily on the panting horse, I felt relaxed, off-guard. "Are you always this competitive?"

"Always."

Suddenly realizing I'd overstepped the mark, I said hastily, "Sorry, I shouldn't have said that."

"Why not?"

"It was rude ... you might think I was criticizing you in some way."

Lee gave a low, smoky chuckle. "Were you?"

"No, of course not." Her amused stare prodded me into saying too much. "I mean ... I think I'm just as competitive as you are, but I don't show it ..."

"Now you're accusing me of being obvious."

I was immediately irritated. *This woman's just playing with me. She knows I'm supposed to keep her happy, but I'm damned if I'll apologize again ...*

To my relief I saw the other riders appearing at the far end of the beach. "I'm going to meet them," I said, nudging my horse with my heels. Her ironic acknowledging nod stayed in my mind as the bay trotted back along the sand.

I'd been warned Lee Paynter was hard, demanding and difficult to please — so why in the hell was I verbally jousting with her? Ruefully I considered the possibilities. Perhaps it was an unconscious career death-wish. Or perhaps my resentment was based on envy of her self-assurance.

When possible, Sir Frederick scheduled a brief morning staff meeting each day of a convention, and he frowned upon latecomers. In the space of forty minutes I had seen Lee back to her cabana, showered, changed into white shorts and a hot pink

32

top, pinned on my green and gold identification badge, and hurried to join the twenty or so A.P.P. staff in the administration block meeting room.

Sharon Castell and Steve Monahan waved to me, indicating they'd saved me a seat, but before I could take it Sir Frederick called me over. "Alexandra, I noticed you left last night's dinner rather early ..."

Surprised I'd been missed in such a seafood spectacular, I said, "I'm sorry, Sir Frederick, I was tired, so I took the opportunity to slip away. Was there something you needed me for?"

He patted my arm. "A few things, but they'll wait. How are you getting on with Lee Paynter?"

"Fine."

His expression indicated he expected a more detailed response, so I added, "Very well. We went horseback-riding this morning."

"Excellent. But if you have any problems or worries, Alexandra, I want you to come straight to me. Her good will is very important, as you know."

When I joined the others, Steve, looking more than ever the stereotypical Aussie male, said with satisfaction, "I told you Sir Fred was interested — he can't keep his hands off you."

I stared at him.

"Don't bother glaring at me, Alex," he went on, "because I'm sure Sharon agrees with me."

Sharon rolled her eyes. To change the subject, I said to her, "Saw you hitting off this morning. Good game?"

"It was great, though I lost a ball in the rainforest."

"Lee Paynter wants to play golf, and I'm not up to her standard — I just hack my way around a

33

course. Is there a chance you could fit in with her schedule?"

Sharon made an expansive gesture. "Anything to please the customers. I'll look her up and make a definite time."

I smiled at her, reflecting on how much I valued our firm but undemanding friendship. A large woman, both physically and in extroverted manner, Sharon Castell had a smile so wide and white that it seemed she had been blessed with more than the usual number of teeth. Flaming red hair sprang from her scalp in thick, irrepressible waves. People responded positively to her genuine warmth. Not only was I fond of Sharon, I admired her professionally. She was the consummate publicist, and her association with Australasian Pan Pacific had done much to ensure the convention's influential guest list. It seemed to me she was on a first-name basis with almost everybody who was anybody, but this easy familiarity gave no impression of opportunism or expediency.

Sir Frederick had positioned himself behind the lectern on the dais. He tapped sharply for attention, waited until the babble of conversation became a respectful silence, then began the meeting. He was dapper in what I call English Gentlemen's Tropical Wear — a tailored cream safari shirt with silk cravat, tan shorts ending just above the knee, matching long socks and soft leather slip-on shoes. The finishing touch to the outfit lay on a table — a cream-colored panama hat decorated with a band of the same material as his cravat.

Although it was a ridiculous idea, I considered

34

Steve's suggestion that Sir Frederick might be interested in me at a personal level. He was a widower, his wife, a respected but genteel novelist, having died two years previously. I supposed some would consider him a worthy catch — a title, money and membership in the social elite, combined with a well-preserved body, distinguished bearing and a hearty manner. I grinned to myself. Was it really conceivable that Sir Frederick saw me as the future Lady Alexandra?

Steve had been watching me. He pressed his elbow against my ribs. "Considering the possibilities, eh?"

Sir Frederick paused, obviously irritated that anyone should be speaking during his address. He waited long enough to make the point, then concluded his succinct comments on the day's activities.

As printed schedules were distributed by Jackie Luff, his sharp-featured personal assistant, Sir Frederick closed with his usual rah rah exhortation to the troops: "And I'm sure I don't need to remind you that our guests are very influential people. I want them to enjoy every moment, and leave with a more than favorable view of Australia. We're here to make sure they know what our country has to offer their clients — not only some of the most spectacular scenery in the world, but also our way of doing things in a relaxed, friendly but efficient manner."

It was characteristic of his speaking style that he waited for a few moments for this to sink in, then he concluded, "And lastly, we are all here to make things run smoothly, to promote Australasian tourism, and, of course, to have a good time ourselves."

Steve snorted. "Have a good time? I'm flat out just keeping up." He nudged me again. "But speaking of good times, how are you going with Lee Paynter?"

"Steve, would you keep your elbow to yourself?"

He ignored my complaint, saying in a jocular tone, "She's got a rep as a fast worker. Loves 'em and leaves 'em — you know how it is." His grin had an edge of malice to it. "Put the hard word on you yet?"

Sharon raised her eyebrows, but I didn't allow my expression to change. "Not yet. And quite unlikely to, Steve."

He went on facetiously, "Well, love, if *you're* not her cup of tea, watch out you don't find yourself scouting out talent on her behalf. Remember Sir Frederick wants her kept particularly happy ..." ·

I'd had enough. "You see me as a pimp, do you, Steve?"

He blinked. I wasn't playing the game the way he wanted it played. "Oh, fair go, Alex. It was only a joke."

"I'm not laughing."

Steve hated to be at a disadvantage, so he seized the initiative again. "Lee Paynter's not a bad looker, *and* she wouldn't be short of a quid. Pity it's all wasted."

Although experience had taught me that the best course was to ignore him, I couldn't resist. "You're saying all this because she's never shown the slightest interest in *you.*"

36

Sharon had been listening to us with a cynical smile. "You tell him, kid," she said to me.

He wasn't offended by my remark, only amused. "Too true, love, too true." He added with a half-joking leer, "Bet I could straighten her out, given half the chance."

Sharon hooted. "Don't tell me — let me guess. Just one wonderful night with you is all it takes. Right?"

"Right. A good screw's what she needs — and I'm the man to do it."

Sharon chuckled at my response to this: "I'll be sure to tell her. No doubt she'll be captivated by your offer."

"Steve's just stirring," said Sharon after he left us. "Don't let him get to you . . . it's his idea of fun."

I shrugged. I could hardly have been less interested in Steve or his motivations. However, it was a different story with my American charge. "Sharon, how well do you know Lee Paynter?"

"As well as anybody in the business, I suppose. I don't think many people get close to her."

"And?"

"And she's great. I like her."

I smiled at her affectionately. "Sharon, you like everybody. It's your job."

"Yes, but I really do like Lee. She can be brash, she drives a hard bargain, but she's got integrity."

"I'm supposed to look after her. It'd help if I knew a bit more. All I hear is that she's charming but basically ruthless, and she has a reputation for being difficult."

Sharon grinned. "If Lee'd been a male, she'd be admired for her single-minded drive and disciplined

37

approach. Since she's a woman, she's ruthless and difficult."

"So what do you know about this ruthless, difficult woman?"

Sharon flung her arms wide. "Gossip? Or just the facts?"

I put a hand on her shoulder, aware as I did so how rare it was for me to make even casual physical contact. "Whatever you want to tell me. Come on, I'll buy you a cup of coffee and you can give me the lowdown."

The Tern Island Coffee Shop notable, but not for coffee alone — it provided a selection of exotic tortes, tarts, cakes and pastries that made adherence to a diet a heroic exercise. Sharon, announcing that self-denial was damaging to the character, chose a slice of what seemed to be the stickiest and richest of chocolate confections sitting fatly in the refrigerated cabinet. I'd never developed a taste for sweet things — my parents had strictly limited such frivolity when I was young — so I chose cheese and crackers.

Sharon looked sympathetically at my plate. "You need to indulge yourself now and then, Alex. It's no fun being a puritan all the time."

This remark drew a laughing protest from me. "I'm not."

Sharon didn't smile. "You're so hard on yourself. You seem to set rules and regulations to live by. When do you give yourself room to play?"

This wasn't a comfortable conversation, particularly since her summation of people was always unnervingly accurate. "Enough of me," I said lightly. "Let's have the info on Lee Paynter."

Sharon reflected as she took a large bite out of her cake. "Okay, here we have a very successful woman, and she didn't get there by playing Ms. Nice Guy. Hence all these remarks hinting she's a ball-breaking bitch."

"I haven't heard anyone be that extreme ..."

"Sure you have, you just haven't recognized it. Steve's a good example. And he's doubly threatened by the fact she's openly gay. That means she can't be intimidated sexually, or encouraged to play the role of little woman."

I was astonished at the underlying anger in Sharon's voice. "I didn't realize you felt this way."

She ran her hands through her mane of red hair. "I'm in publicity. I like everyone, remember?" She went on more seriously, "You must know what it's like. You just can't rest on your laurels — you have to keep on proving you're better than the male competition. And at the same time, be careful not to reveal anything that could be categorized as feminine weakness. Isn't that true?"

I shrugged. "Suppose so."

"Lee Paynter's opted not to climb the corporate ladder, but to run her own company. Even so, she still has to deal with businesses run by men who resent powerful women."

Suddenly I felt bleak. "It's all bloody depressing."

"No, it isn't. Not when women like Lee make it to the top. And she didn't inherit a business from family or husband, she built it all herself."

"So, what's she like as a person?"

Thoughtfully, Sharon stirred sugar into her cappuccino. "I think there's a lot more to her than meets the eye, but she's not the sort to show it.

Plenty of gossip about her, of course, since she's so openly a lesbian. For what it's worth, I've heard she plays the field. First time I met her socially she was with one woman, and a week later, it was another one, so I guess there's some truth in it. Having said that, I've got to say she never mixes business with pleasure. As you can imagine, there'd be some who'd be delighted to spread gossip accusing her of sexual harassment."

She paused to sip her coffee. "So, is this what you want?"

I felt uncomfortable, wondering if this discussion of the woman's personal life *was* what I wanted. I cleared my throat. "Her business is successful ..."

"So it should be. Basically, Lee Paynter knows what she wants, and most of the time, she gets it." Sharon grinned as she added, "But in case you're worried, no matter what Steve says, I've never heard that she makes a move on anyone who isn't gay ..."

I said mockingly, "And you know how I like to live life to the fullest."

One thing that sets Tern Island apart is that it has its own colony of artists. The group was founded by an eccentric potter some years ago and is now well established in a patch of rainforest within comfortable walking distance from the beach. It's a symbiotic arrangement: the resort's brochures describe the colony as an exotic addition to the usual offerings of tropical paradises; the craft workers and artists flog their work to curious visitors.

Sir Frederick himself joined our party of ten or so guests scheduled for a morning inspection of the craft center and its merchandise. Hilary Ferguson, looking splendid but inappropriate in a chic cream safari outfit, chatted to him for a few moments. I thought how alien their cool English accents sounded in the hot tropical environment. Then Sir Frederick said a few words to me about arrangements for chartered helicopters to visit Cape Tribulation.

When he strode to the front of the group I was irresistibly reminded of a prefect about to start a school excursion. We set off, obediently following his lead, the clipped words of his English accent floating back as he enthused to a particularly important Japanese tour organizer.

"Our Fred's wooing the yen," said Steve as he caught up to me. Today he was wearing a jungle green version of his Aussie outfit, and I glanced at his belt, almost expecting to see a machete, or at the very least, a large knife. "Where's Lee?" he said.

"Ahead of us. She's talking to the Russian delegate."

"See, she never misses a trick. It's going to be open slather now that what was the communist world is opening wide up to tourism — and she's getting in early."

He broke off as we came up to Lee, who was waiting by the side of the path. Steve gave her his special, little-boy smile. "G'day," he said expansively. "Alex looking after you well, I hope?"

"Of course." I was amused at her raised eyebrow, her air of polite astonishment that he should ask such a question.

41

He said uncertainly, "Oh, good." Then, adding a cheerful, "See you later," he dropped back in the group to join Hilary Ferguson.

Lee said, "He's a little condescending, perhaps?"

"Just a little," I said drily, and her mouth quirked.

The air was permeated with the moist heavy smell of decay and the ceaseless hum of insects. The path to the craft center led over a swinging rope-and-plank bridge spanning a gully so choked with growth that it was impossible to see how deep it actually was. After crossing the bridge the trail twisted and turned to avoid huge exposed roots and massive tree trunks. Overhead the crowding trees effectively shut out most of the sun, so that ferns and palms — pampered potplants in cooler climates — grew wild, springing with enormous vigor from the layers of rotting leaves and bark. Looking almost theatrical, fat vines hung in huge loops from the trees they were strangling.

"I'd hardly be surprised to see Tarzan go swinging by," said Lee. Looking sideways at me, she added, "Or preferably, Jane."

I smiled briefly, wondering what, if anything, she thought of me. Did she assume I was heterosexual? Or perhaps she sensed the truth, that sex wasn't really very important to me. That I was essentially uninterested.

Her American cadences broke into my thoughts. "I've discussed with Sir Frederick the concept of eco-tours to unspoiled areas American tourists wouldn't ordinarily see."

"Soft adventures?" This industry term delighted

me, summing up, as it did, the idea of daring combined with comfort.

"Not necessarily so soft. Some of us are willing to do without a hot shower every day. Sir Frederick said you'd have some suggestions. What I'd like is detailed itineraries of possible mini-tours that could be options together with assessments of ground operators active in the areas. Okay?"

"When would you like this?"

"As soon as possible."

I smiled assent, but my thoughts were sour. Of course she wanted everything as soon as possible. What Lee Paynter demanded, Lee Paynter got. I allowed myself the luxury of feeling put-upon, then I had to admit the unpalatable truth — I was just looking for something to dislike about her. It wasn't the perfectly reasonable request to supply tour information that had made me defensive, it was her openness about her sexuality that grated.

My mother's voice, soft yet biting, echoed from the past: "People are talking, Alex. They're saying dirty, disgusting things about you and Zoe. Unthinkable things ..."

My absorption in my thoughts had carried me, unheeding to the craft center. I surveyed the theatrical scene, thinking derisively that it was just *too* artistic. The rainforest had been cleared so that a splash of sunlight poured in to spotlight the various sculptures surrounding the focus of attention, a huge and brilliantly colored birdbath. The main building, constructed of stained wooden planks wrapped in a shawl of flowering creepers, had a steeply sloping roof inset with a series of stained-glass skylights. Along the ridge were several fantastic windvanes, many a combination of driftwood and enameled metals.

A heavily bearded man appeared, his pink smock at war with his ginger hair. This was Malcolm, the principal artisan of the colony. I'd heard his presentation before and admired the way his carefully rehearsed patter sounded spontaneous.

He led us inside to the crafts. There was a wide range of them — leatherwork, pottery, hand-woven and embroidered clothing, paintings, carved wooden artifacts, jewelry and enamelware. Some of it was particularly beautiful, especially a display of silver jewelry that incorporated semi-precious stones, small pieces of coral and tiny shells.

Irrelevantly, I wondered which piece I'd choose for Lee, and had picked out a silver and coral necklace before I realized it was ridiculous for me to be selecting jewelry for a stranger.

I'll be knitting her a jumper, next!

I smiled. Lee, of course, would call it a sweater.

Then I was angry with myself. The woman was obviously getting to me — and this in less than two days. And, disconcertingly, I found I was aware of exactly where she was — I didn't have to look — I knew she was behind me and to my left, deep in conversation with the bearded Malcolm.

Unobtrusively I moved closer. She was discussing craft items she thought would be of particular interest to American visitors and the arrangements that could be made for the dispatch of larger articles to the States.

I made an effort to view her objectively. She looked and sounded smart and confident. There was an alert, no-nonsense air about her, but also a real charm. When she listened it was with close attention, her body language indicating her concentration on the other person, as though no one else at that moment could possibly say anything of greater interest. And when she spoke her voice was warm, full of vitality and sincerity.

From his enthusiastic response it was clear that Malcolm was completely disarmed by Lee, but as a detached observer, I could say to myself: *I'm* not disarmed. I'm not susceptible to this woman's charisma.

Tony Englert settled his ample form into an office chair with a sigh. "Alex, my darling, I'm fed up to here with the beauties of our wondrous land." He leveled his hand at nose height.

Grinning at his doleful tone, I said, "You've got a touch of conventionitis. It'll pass. Trust me. I know."

He closed his eyes with exaggerated weariness. "It's okay for *you* to say that — at least you get to *do* something. I just trail round after Sir Frederick, being indispensable. It's not a laugh a minute." He opened his eyes. "Incidentally, he *is* showing a keen interest in your career ..."

"Sir Frederick?"

"The very one."

"What is this?" I said, feeling a mixture of resistance and impatience. "A conspiracy? I suppose you've been listening to Steve Monahan's version of events."

Tony's expression changed. He said viciously,

"That bastard? I'd just love to have him come a gutser over something."

I was astonished. I'd never heard Tony speak with such venom before. "What's Steve done to you?"

He sat up straight, his face resuming his usual pleasant expression. "Nothing worth worrying about."

His tone made it obvious the subject was to be dropped, so I said, "Lee Paynter's asked for outlines of possible eco-tours. I get the idea she wants sort of hard-soft adventures."

"What about our Adventurer Package?"

Tony was referring to an additional package A.P.P. had devised as suggested add-ons for fit and venturesome under thirty-fives — strenuous and sometimes dangerous activities like white water rafting in Tasmania, roughing it in Arnhem Land, going caving in sinkholes near Margaret River in Western Australia. "Too tough," I said. "These are going to be ordinary tourists who want to see something different and challenging, but they don't want to be too uncomfortable. Any suggestions?"

"Sure. Broome and the Kimberley region for one. Yes? And how about Shark Bay? It's World Heritage listed, stunningly beautiful, and in the middle of nowhere. How am I doing?"

Suddenly swept with a wave of affection, I resisted the impulse to lean over and touch him. "An adequate effort," I said mockingly, wondering what the hell was wrong with me. Good old self-contained Alex was on the verge of being — horror of horrors — demonstrative.

CHAPTER FOUR

Before the next day's briefing, as Sharon took the chair next to me she said, "Had my golf game with Lee early this morning. She asked about you — a sort of subtle cross-examination."

"Oh?"

Sharon grinned. "You can sound as offhand as you like — I know you're just dying to find out just what I said about you."

I sat forward, intrigued. "I'm more interested in what Lee Paynter wanted to know, and why."

"I think it's normal for her ... she likes to get

the good oil on everybody she deals with. That's part of why she's successful."

Quite aware that Sharon was teasing me, I still couldn't resist asking, "So what *did* you say about me?"

She said with irony, "Only the truth, Alex, although I must say most people don't act as though the truth is necessarily in their best interests."

The truth? That was too close to home. I couldn't prevent the edge in my voice. "What's your version of the truth?"

She looked at me sharply. "Are you angry? I thought you'd be pleased she's taking an interest in you as a person, and not just as an A.P.P. employee."

"I'm ecstatic."

"Now, Alex, don't be like that. I'll tell you exactly what I told her." She chuckled. "More or less — I don't want you getting a swelled head."

I waited patiently, knowing it was useless to hurry Sharon when she was in a jocular mood. When it became obvious I wasn't going to respond, she went on, "Lee said you had impressed her, particularly, I might say, on the tennis court. She asked about your background and how you happened to join A.P.P. I gave a sketchy outline of your career as I knew it, said you were on the way up, mentioned that I valued your friendship ... all that sort of laudatory stuff."

I didn't mean to put the question into words, but curiosity got the better of me. "Did she ask if I was married?"

"As a matter of fact, she did. I mentioned you were divorced. Is that okay?"

Our conversation stopped as Sir Frederick tapped the lectern for silence. His assistant, Jackie, glared around the room on his behalf, directing a particularly virulent glance in our direction. She didn't like me, that I knew, but why and when this antipathy towards me had started was a puzzle.

Sir Frederick began speaking, but I hardly heard what he said, my thoughts dwelling with irritation, even resentment, on the fact that Lee Paynter had asked personal questions — and that Sharon had answered them.

I sighed to myself, admitting that I'd done exactly the same when asking for information about Lee Paynter, so self-righteousness was hardly in order. Of course, I could always rationalize my interest — knowing what made people tick was an important part of good management.

So on both sides it was a professional interest. No more than that.

Steve and I were to accompany eighteen guests on the brief flight to Cairns, then half of the party would go with me on a catamaran ferry out to the Barrier Reef while Steve and the other nine boarded a game-fishing launch to hunt black marlin. The special flight for Cairns left immediately after the meeting, so I'd arranged for a mini-bus to collect the guests and then to pick us up from the briefing.

The bus arrived, Steve boarding with much good cheer and "G'days," and I followed more soberly. There was a vacant seat next to Lee so I took it. "Enjoy your golf this morning?"

"Sure. Sharon's quite a competitor." Then, seeming to sense there might be something more to my question, she added with a slight smile, "And perhaps she's mentioned that I asked about you."

I kept my face blank. *Why is she so bloody direct? Is it to put me at a disadvantage?* "She did say something . . ."

Lee answered the implied question. "I'm interested."

I felt an unexpected, unwanted twinge of excitement — and relief that we'd arrived at the airport and I didn't have to respond.

The pilot, cheerfully calling everyone of either sex "Mate," loaded hand-luggage while Steve and I shuffled everyone into the cramped cabin. I was amused to see he was careful to make sure Hilary Ferguson boarded after the front seats were full, so that he could sit near her. Within a few minutes we were ready, the little plane gave a few preparatory shudders, then roared importantly down the airstrip and bounced into the pale blue sky.

I'd made sure not to sit too close to Lee ... I wanted to examine the surprising pleasure her interest had caused me.

The loud monotone of the engine made conversation difficult, and the German delegate beside me spoke with a heavy accent that matched his Teutonic bulk, so it was easy to give up any pretense of conversation. He had a window seat, and having pointed out a few items of interest, I felt my duty had been done for the moment, and I could relax.

I hated being labeled like a parcel, so I took the opportunity of removing my green and gold name tag. Sir Frederick had the irritating habit of doing lightning checks of tag-wearing and to miscreants he would always say the same thing: "Your name is important! No one must ever doubt who you are and the purpose for which you're there. It's a reminder to *you,* as well as to our guests."

I stretched my legs as far as possible in the cramped seating and tried to release the tension in my shoulders. Lee was in my favorite seat directly behind the pilot and peered over his shoulder at the island-dotted water below. I looked at her reflectively. She was not someone who could be ignored. Perhaps it was her aura of energy, of purpose . . .

As in the dining room, she seemed to sense that she was being watched. She turned her head, catching me before I could look away. For a moment our eyes met with curious intensity, then Otto, my large German companion, plucked at my arm with a question, and I broke the link to answer him.

Cairns, sprawling along the shore of Trinity Bay, is surrounded by plantations of sugar cane, pineapple and macadamia, each adding its own distinctive green to the patchwork of the land. In the bay itself countless vessels nestle against the shore, or, like toys in a pond, make their way in or out of the inlet.

As the plane sank towards the runway, I glanced inland. Passive under fat white clouds, crumpled green hills delineated the rich coastal strip. At times like this, when I'm on the edge of our huge continent, yet disconnected from the ground, I'm always conscious of the Center — that immense and mysterious heart of Australia — the Outback.

As usual, Cairns was imbued with an atmosphere of freedom and good times, its luxury hotels, bars, restaurants and shops there to tempt the city's lifeblood — tourists. The sun danced on the turquoise water as Steve took his mainly male group towards Marlin Jetty where sleek lethal-looking vessels waited to take the hunters of black marlin, sharks and barracudas out into the Coral Sea.

I grimaced as I watched them go. The year before I'd had a "famil" — a familiarization trip on one of the game-fishing boats. The guest of honor was a loud-mouthed television star who had, with unobtrusive assistance from the crew, hooked a gigantic marlin. Handling the heavy tackle with great difficulty, he had sweated and bellowed as the fish fought ferociously for its life. He hadn't been able to finish the exercise, being too unfit, so one of the crew had taken over. I could still see his smug, proud huntsman-with-prey smile as he posed on the dock with the massive marlin dangling beside him, still beautiful in death.

Green Island, our destination, was a low coral cay on the Great Barrier Reef, less than an hour from Cairns. The catamaran ferry, burnished aluminum and blue trim, scudded along, leaving a froth of white on the iridescent water. I felt joyously alive. The scent of the sea, the whoosh of the vessel through the water, the taste of salt on my lips, the warm, lazy promise of the breeze — all these filled me with elation.

I surveyed my group: a Canadian man, thin and intense; my large German friend, Otto; two women from Britain — one the beautiful Hilary, stunning in white with a large hat protecting her peaches-and-cream complexion — the other an angular Scot with a lilting Western Highlands accent and a no-nonsense air; a bubbly woman from Ireland who actually said "begorrah"; two Scandinavian men, both fitting the stereotype of blond hair and blue eyes; a very consciously macho man from Argentina who displayed elaborate courtesy to every woman and a suspicious glare to every man.

And Lee.

I organized drinks and snacks, answered questions and generally mother-henned until the delegates spread themselves throughout the vessel, relaxing in conversation or just enjoying the scenery. But not Lee. She prowled restlessly, checking out the catamaran from bow to stern and then spending some time in discussion with the captain. I smiled at her when she finally came down to the lower deck. "Everything satisfactory?"

It seems she might be willing, at last, to relax. She stretched luxuriously. "Very much so." She gestured towards the low green lines of the island we were rapidly approaching. "And I guess I'm about to see a little more of paradise."

Compared to Tern Island, tiny Green Island is insignificant. Thousands of years of eddying water have built the little cay from the accumulated sediments of its platform reef, so that it now crowns the living coral with an oval cap of lush vegetation. And I've always thought Green Island an unnecessarily pedestrian name that gives no hint of the enchanting undersea world around it.

We were to have two hours on the island, and then travel further east to the outer edge of the Great Barrier Reef. There was little for me to do, as the members of the group were quite accustomed to assessing tourist attractions without guidance, but I made sure that everyone entered the underwater observatory, which was set into the jetty where we had docked.

As we looked through the thick plate glass at the alien beauty of the undersea world, it amused me to consider the reversal in roles: humans captive in an air-filled tank, while fish swam freely.

Lee was captivated. When I joined her at one of the windows she touched my arm as she said, "This is wonderful."

It was only a brush of fingers, but I was acutely conscious of the contact. I resisted the impulse to rub my skin to remove the tingle, instead concentrating on the microcosm beyond the glass. Coral, starfish, anemones — familiar from brochures and photographs but now so much more vividly real in their world of filtered green light. In colors and patterns like delicious marine confections, tropical fish darted in precision underwater ballets, or eyed us thoughtfully while gliding past. I could provide some of their names — the Imperial Angel fish with its gaudy yellow stripes, the green and blue Parrot fish, the conspicuous red bands of the Red Emperor, the yellow black and white of the tiny, but gorgeous, Moorish Idol.

I reminded the group that because of low tide it would be possible to walk out onto the reef itself, that there were glass-bottomed boats available and we would meet for lunch at twelve.

Lee took a last look at a school of tiny luminous fish zig-zagging in accurate formation, each member apparently preprogrammed in a series of intricate moves. Then she said briskly, "I want to check out the island."

She was as good as her word. This was no leisurely stroll and I certainly had no time to stand and admire the contrast between the white coral sand, the twisted gray-white shapes of driftwood and the depthless azure of the sky. Wearing sand-shoes to protect our feet from the sharp cutting edges, we walked out onto the extensive area of exposed reef. Lee was interested in everything, quizzing with implacable persistence and charm a resident naturalist about the breeding habits of coral polyps, the gourmet food possibilities of the beche-de-mer or sea cucumber, the destructive capabilities of the crown-of-thorns starfish, the likelihood of standing on a deadly stonefish, and whether the open jaws of giant clams could close and trap a swimmer by an unwary foot. He laughed at her last question, saying, "Great story — pity about the facts ..."

It was the same routine with the glass-bottomed boats. Lee peppered our guide with questions while we floated over coral that glowed in vibrant colors. The massive solid growths were in shades of purple, mauve, yellow and brown. The delicate branching corals were bright in pink, green and yellow. This underwater world was teeming with life: red and white spotted reef crabs, brilliant blue starfish, orange and black brittle stars, shoals of luminous fish, red and pink anemones with their little companion fish lurking, unharmed, amongst the poisonous tentacles; frilled sea slugs, slate-pencil sea urchins, blue spotted rays. And shells — tiger cowries, cloth-of-gold cones and spider shells, helmet shells, bailer shells and, most fascinating to me, the giant clams, lying with their valves apart to show their beautiful velvet mantles in shades of dark green through to peacock blue.

Lee was still asking questions during the sumptuous smorgasbord lunch aboard the catamaran. While the rest of us ate with keen appetites, she queried the staff about catering arrangements.

"You *could* relax for a few minutes," I suggested, lulled into unguarded mildness by a glass of wine.

"I could — but I'm not here to enjoy myself. This is business."

I felt a flash of dislike for this intense, brusque woman. Acknowledging her with a cool nod, I turned away, promising myself that in future I'd be careful not to overstep the invisible line. I'll think of myself as a paid companion, I thought savagely.

The sun was brilliant on the water, but some of the delight had gone from the day, and I felt remote from the loveliness of the little lonely cays. Our destination on the edge of the Great Barrier Reef was one of the myriad of individual reefs that together made the longest living entity in the world — two thousand kilometers of tiny coral polyps, a thin veneer of life building upon foundations created by the countless skeletons of their forerunners.

As we moored at the outer reef, Hilary exclaimed, "Is that a turtle?"

She was pointing at a half-submerged greenish dome which, as we watched, sank below the surface. So clear was the water, however, that we could see the turtle's outstretched head and the beat of its powerful flippers as it pursued a school of fish. One of the two marine biologists who had joined our party at Green Island was obviously pleased at the opportunity to get to know Hilary better. Although he raised his voice so we all could hear, his smiling attention was directed at her attractive face. "It's a green turtle, and fully grown. Its carapace is about a meter long — a bit over three feet — and it weighs around a hundred and twenty kilos, or three hundred pounds. They spend their lives in the water, and only the females ever have to drag that weight onto the sand, and that's to lay their eggs."

"Typical!" said Hilary. "It's always the women who have to do the hard work."

Lee grinned at me. "Ain't that the truth?"

I returned her smile, feeling more comfortable with her. Perhaps I was becoming accustomed to the abrasive surface of her personality.

There was a choice of activities at the reef — snorkeling, scuba diving and viewing from semi-submersibles. Those who'd be swimming went to the changing cabins to get into bathing costumes — I was already wearing my bikini under my clothes — and we then assembled to be given instructions and equipment. The group split up into twos and threes and I was not surprised to see the darkly handsome Argentine make sure he accompanied Hilary Ferguson.

With amused irritation I learned that Lee was a certified scuba diver. It would be a relief to find there was *something* she didn't do well.

I said mildly, "I'll just be snorkeling, Lee — scuba diving isn't one of my skills."

"Then I'll snorkel with you."

Her statement warmed me, but I swiftly doused this with cold common sense. No way was this woman making a line for me. She didn't mix business with pleasure; I hadn't indicated the slightest interest; it was unlikely I was her type, anyway.

And, Alex, you don't want a repeat of last time . . .

The cold deep blue of the open ocean broke its swells against the thickness of the reef structure, but inside that fortress the water was green and tepid. Fitting on our flippers, masks and snorkels, we slipped into the water — a far less heroic entrance than the resounding splashes the scuba divers made.

I was soon lost in the discoveries of the underwater world and the profusion of marine plants and animals who made these porous ramparts their home. Through the forests of coral — delicate staghorn, honeycomb, round-head — the bright bodies of tropical fish flashed and darted.

We swam along with Blue Tang fish, admired the elaborately frilled Butterfly Cod, watched exquisite little blue-green Demoiselles hover then dash away, avoided the sinister slow-flapping progress of a Stingaree ray, swooped over the waving tentacles of anemones and at one point I touched Lee's shoulder to point out a banded coral shrimp picking parasites and fungus from the body of a yellow striped reef fish who remained still while this extraordinary cleaning was going on.

Even after several hours, Lee was reluctant to leave, although we were the last in the water. Clinging to the metal ladder on the side of the catamaran, she stripped off her mask to say, "I haven't seen enough. It's like a huge underwater garden. I could stay in it much longer."

I began to clamber up the ladder. "Careful, you might fall behind in your schedule," I said.

Lee laughed up at me. "I'm sure I deserved that, Alex. My staff often say I'm impossible."

She swung herself onto the deck, accepting a glass of fruit juice and a towel from a crew member who smiled appreciatively as he gave her the once-over. I went to get changed as she joined Hilary on the outside front deck for a last view of the outer reef.

As I toweled my hair dry I felt a familiar emptiness. So often, when the main activity of a day was over, my essential solitariness would overwhelm me, and I'd have to resist sinking into the self-indulgence of a melancholy mood.

The main area of the catamaran held a central bar with tables and upholstered bench seats set along the expanse of windows on both sides. Reef exploration was thirsty work — those who weren't clustered around the bar had taken their drinks to convenient tables. I'd done one obligatory circuit, smiling dutifully, when Lee appeared fully dressed. "Join me, Alex?"

I had white wine; she settled for bourbon. She'd obviously put her investigative side on hold, and was prepared to relax. Lounging with drink in hand, she contemplated me over the rim of her glass. "What is it you like best about your job?"

I usually consider a question before I give an answer, but this time I responded immediately. "I love my country — it's beautiful. I love showing it off to other people. Frankly, I love my job." I stopped, embarrassed. "Sorry. That sounded a bit schmaltzy, didn't it?"

Lee's smile had a warmth I hadn't seen before. "No, it didn't."

"How about you? What do you like best about what you do?"

"Being the boss. Running my own business. Living with my successes — and my mistakes."

I wanted to keep her like this, open and unguarded. "You sound like you really get a charge out of it."

She sat forward, alive with enthusiasm. "I sure do. I started as a little one-person travel agency then I extended, borrowed money, took chances, started running my own tours to South America. Those first few years, I could have folded any minute. Luck and ignorance kept me going. It was so exciting, knowing decisions I made would make or break me — I couldn't blame anyone else if things went bad."

Looking at her animated face, I felt a pang of envy. To care so much about something, to relish the rewards with such ardor. "Is it still so exciting?"

"Yes, but it's different. It's not just me against the world, now. The business has grown, and I wholesale my tours to other operators. I've got a lot of people working for me, so if I sink, so do they."

"You don't have a partner?"

Lee raised her eyebrows. "A partner? Oh, I see, you mean in the business ..."

I could feel myself blushing at the misunderstanding. Angry because I felt at a disadvantage, I said sharply, "Of course I mean a business partner. Why would you think I'd be asking you a question about your personal life?"

"Because you're curious."

There was a silence I had to fill. I said, "Can I get you another drink?"

Lee kept eye contact as she handed me her glass. "Thank you."

Aware that she was watching me, I walked to the catamaran's central bar with as much nonchalance as possible. What did I feel? A sort of angry excitement. The anger I understood; the excitement alarmed me.

That night I dreamed of my dead brother. Bobby had drowned when he was ten. In my dream I was six again and we were on the beach that hot, sunny, terrible day. I saw everything as if I were hovering above the action. Curling white lines of surf rolled forcefully onto the shore, the water was crowded with bobbing heads, and my brother waded out to meet the waves, my father behind him. My mother sat reading under the shade of a beach umbrella and I could see myself playing at the edge of the surf, resisting the receding water as it tried to pull me out of my depth. Then, at the place where the body surfers caught the waves — the collapse of the sandbank, the rip sweeping dozens of swimmers out to sea, the screams for help . . .

My six-year-old self, crying in uncomprehending terror, as my brother's body was carried up the beach by lifeguards . . . The frantic attempts to revive him . . . My father crouched in the sand covering his face with his hands . . . My mother saying over and over, "Bobby, Bobby — why *you*? Why *you*?"

I woke, shivering and crying, as I had shivered and cried that summer day. No one had comforted me then; no one was here to comfort me now. I turned on the light, got out of bed, walked aimlessly around the room — anything to dispel the dark weight of memories. As an adult, I could see that Bobby's death had soured and then destroyed my mother's delight in life. She had adored him, and when he died the center of her seemed to fade and wither.

My parents never put it into words, but I grew to suspect, and finally to accept, that if *I* had died the loss to the family — to my mother — would have been less.

To be fair, my childhood had not been unhappy. In their own way my parents had loved me and they had never stinted me anything. It was just that no matter how hard I tried, I knew that for them I was second best.

CHAPTER FIVE

The next morning I stood with Sir Frederick on the pier discussing possibilities for the additional mini-tours Lee had requested. My white slacks and tangerine shirt seemed too informal next to his impeccable yachting outfit, which included a dark blue blazer with an exclusive private club's insignia on the pocket. But he said, "You look particularly charming this morning, Alexandra."

I murmured a thank you, aware that this was an unusually personal remark. Rather more disturbingly, he hadn't commented on the fact that I'd forgotten my name badge. Steve's dire warnings and Tony's dry comments suddenly seemed to have some currency.

Members of a select group chosen to spend an overnight cruise with Sir Frederick on a converted pearling schooner were arriving. The boat had been extensively refitted to provide leisurely luxury tours of the Barrier Reef and coastal islands. Gleaming white, its previous life as a hard-working commercial craft obliterated, the *Ocean Dream,* complete with chef, marine biologist and the accoutrements of opulent living, rocked gently as Tony Englert assisted guests aboard.

Sir Frederick frowned over the list of hard-soft adventures I'd drawn up at Lee's request. "The Flinders Ranges and the Warrumbungles are both good choices. In Western Australia I'd include Wittenoom Gorge and the Pinnacles, as well as Broome and the Kiberley region. Contact Sydney office and tell them exactly what you want. This has got to be a fast, professional job. By tomorrow afternoon when we return I want Lee to have detailed itineraries, brochures, comparative costs of different operators — and I want it all presented in a complete, professional package. As always, appearance is important." He took my elbow. "I've told Jackie you'll be using my office." His fingers tightened. "I'm relying on you, Alexandra."

Lee walked onto the pier, deep in conversation with Hilary Ferguson. Sir Frederick followed my gaze and smiled broadly as he released me. "Good morning!" He deftly passed Hilary to me, concentrating upon Lee. "We've just been discussing your adventure tours. While we're cruising,

Alexandra will be teeing up the information, so you'll have comprehensive details tomorrow."

Hilary smiled at me sympathetically. "I say, it doesn't seem fair to have you inside working while we're out enjoying this beautiful weather. I'd rather hoped you'd be on the cruise with us."

"Someone has to do the work," said Sir Frederick heartily as he clapped me on the shoulder. I gave the required smile, somewhat alarmed that he'd touched me again. I was resisting the idea that it was personal, not only because it would create a complication I didn't need, but because I didn't want to face Steve's I-told-you-so glee.

Sir Frederick beamed. "You're in good hands, Lee. Alexandra's explored some of the most remote and inhospitable parts of Australia."

Under the circumstances, I couldn't see this was much of a recommendation. "Yes," I said cheerfully, "and I only got lost some of the time."

The weather was perfect, the moon would be full this night, and the *Ocean Dream* was cruising one of the most beautiful seascapes in the world. My errant imagination could picture me standing on the deck in the moonlight, talking softly to Lee Paynter as we passed silvered islands in a silver sea.

This attractive but far-fetched vision was broken by Jackie Luff's penetrating voice. Managing the difficult task of sounding all at once challenging, rude and badly-done-by, she said, "Alex? Sydney office's calling you again. Extension two."

As I picked up the receiver I thanked her,

refusing to acknowledge her dislike by showing a corresponding rudeness. Jackie had a profile so composed of angle it might have been cut with tin-snips. Her elbows, her fingers, even the line of her shoulders, seemed sharp. I had noticed that she spoke to Sir Frederick and others in authority with a keen, brisk tone; however, her voice to those she considered inferior, and this included me, was much more belligerent.

I spent a large part of the day on the telephone or at the fax, and by mid-afternoon had lined up most of the information on flights, accommodation and details of not-to-be-missed sights. Now it was up to Sydney office to turn out the finished product and express it up to Tern Island.

Tired, I relaxed in Sir Frederick's plush desk chair, chin in hands, gazing idly at a print of that engagingly named seabird, the masked booby. My thoughts circled around Lee Paynter — but not too close. I had the uneasy conviction that if I allowed myself any further latitude, my treacherous imagination would entice me into pointless fantasies. Of course, this was all to do with Lee's calm acceptance of her lesbianism ... I could never see myself being so open, so unthreatened by public disclosure.

Images I always tried to repress bubbled into my consciousness. My mother, her usually quiet voice caustic, saying, "So we're to understand that Zoe's your *special* friend, are we?" My father sucking in his cheeks, pursing his lips, contemptuously speculating that Zoe was the real reason I'd divorced Carl.

At the time I was twenty-four. Yet my parents'

censure still reduced me to a child desperate not to be rejected. "I didn't meet Zoe until after the divorce. And no matter what you've been told, we're just friends ..."

The first statement was true. The second a lie.

After Carl, I'd wanted a fresh start. I used the money from the property settlements as down payment on a shabby little house and spent my spare time renovating it. Then, when Frank Harp, an acquaintance of my father's, offered me a job as agent in his rapidly growing company, I'd taken it with alacrity because I'd gone as far as I could at the small tourist agency where I'd gained my first taste for the industry. Frank's company gave me the opportunity to extend my education in tourism, and besides, it was fun working there.

Aussie Affairs had a staff of fifteen and we provided what our publicity called "genuine Aussie experiences." Small tourist groups roughed it in a civilized way at selected sheep or cattle stations, where they learned how to muster cattle, shear sheep, make billy tea, cook a damper in a campfire, sing "Waltzing Matilda" and in general gain some concept of Australian country life.

Zoe was the first person I met when I joined the company. She was older than I, a popular, vivid personality with a loud laugh and extravagant gestures. We became friends. Then one night she asked me back to her flat for dinner. We shared a bottle of wine ... a kiss ... her bed. It was an expert, pleasurable seduction and I was astonished by the magnitude of my response — I'd had no idea passion could consume me with such licentious force. In the following months Zoe taught me both the

67

physical techniques of sex and the rules for subterfuge.

And subterfuge was more than prudent; it was essential. Frank Harp made jeering comments and jokes about faggots, lezzies and queers every single day.

My relationship with Zoe was not emotionally intense. Sure, we liked each other well enough, but we had little in common except for the desire that flared between us. It was sufficient; I'd never felt physical fulfillment like this before and each encounter was a delight to my senses.

And I gained something else of great value — an introduction into a gay world I hardly realized existed. For the first time I could relax and be myself. This period of my life was when I met two of my dearest friends, Trish and Suzie, who had been together for six years, and I began to appreciate the invisible gay network that extends throughout society.

Zoe was firmly in the closet, paranoid about being labeled a lesbian. I still don't know how or why the gossip started, but whatever its beginning, its terrifying power became immediately apparent. First the veiled comments, then the open sneers, then Zoe was called up to see Frank.

"The only way to survive is to deny everything," she'd once said to me, and that's what we did.

Frank didn't ask to see me — he called my father instead. I was, I discovered during the searing scene with my parents, regarded as the "innocent party" whose relative inexperience in life and unhappiness at my divorce had made me easy pickings for a predatory lesbian.

I will always be ashamed of my behavior over Zoe, my craven silence. She admitted nothing, nor did I, but she was the one forced to resign, while I was treated as an immature and rather foolish victim. Although at the time Zoe made it clear she didn't expect it, I know I should have stood up for her. I didn't have the guts — not in the face of my mother's loathing. "You want people to think you're one of *those* women? So everywhere you go someone will whisper behind your back? Is that what you want, Alex?"

My father supported her. "If you want a career, Alex, you won't get very far if word gets around . . ."

Zoe moved interstate, taking a job with a government tourism department. I stayed at Aussie Affairs long enough to let the talk die down, then, using the excuse that I needed to extend my experience further, took a position in the international hospitality industry with the Hilton hotel chain.

I now knew, irrevocably, that I was a lesbian. I also knew there was no way I would risk my career or my family relationships by being openly gay. My loneliness impelled me into a series of covert, fleeting affairs which always ended with my retreat for fear of exposure. I entered them expecting very little — and that's what I'd got. Physical release, sometimes, but never passion. Never a feeling of wholeness.

In the last year or so I'd withdrawn completely, accepting that for the time being I would have to make my life alone. It might be a cold comfort — but it was still a comfort — to accept that without deep ties to anyone I would be immune to unhappiness. If remaining on the periphery meant I wouldn't experience the heights of emotion, I'd also avoid the depths. It seemed to me a fair and reasonable compromise.

Jackie Luff startled me out of my reverie by shoving a fax in front of me. "Anything else you want?" she asked ungraciously.

I shook my head, tempted to ask what her problem was with me. Looking at her pugnacious expression I immediately abandoned the idea. I was too tired for a confrontation that would almost certainly prompt a denial from Jackie that anything was wrong.

The fax was inconsequential. I glanced at it and put it to one side, then leaned back and studied my hands. The lines on my palms were clear, definite.

In Sydney a month ago Tony Englert had encouraged me to have my hand read at a street market. One Saturday morning I'd been in Paddington looking for some small unusual gift for Sharon Castell's birthday when I'd heard his familiar voice.

"Alex, darling. What are you doing here?" He lived locally, in a renovated terrace house. "Come and have your fortune told. I can guarantee the service because Madame Marcia's an old friend."

"Madame Marcia?" I was dubious, to say the least.

He chuckled. "So her real name's Deb Smith. You have to admit Madame Debbie doesn't sound the same."

It was ridiculous, but I felt a prickle of irrational trepidation when the flamboyant Madame Marcia seated me inside her cramped stall, took my hands and peered attentively at each palm. And strangely, apart from the usual generalizations, I now remembered one pronouncement, although it was delivered no more dramatically than all the rest: "I see a change, a great change in your life. It will happen very soon, and it will be like a thunderbolt to you! A thunderbolt!"

I wasn't superstitious and couldn't clearly remember any other prediction Tony's friend had made that morning. I was cynical enough to believe that Madame Marcia had made similar, if not identical, predictions to all her clients, so why should this melodramatic utterance have stuck in my mind?

My parents, particularly my mother, had been contemptuous of fortunetelling of any kind. "The future will come soon enough," she would say, her tone implying that it was unlikely to be welcome when it did arrive. Now I wondered if I'd remembered the fortuneteller's words for a negative reason — I was content with my life and didn't want a change, particularly one that could be described as "a thunderbolt."

Would Lee ever have had her palm read? It was easy to visualize her hands. Long, strong fingers; shaped, unvarnished nails. Hands whose gestures reflected Lee's energy, her bold confidence.

Sharon had said Lee played the field. If that were true, then she, like me, had no permanence in her relationships. But perhaps it wasn't true. Perhaps Lee had one woman for whom she reserved the essential core of herself.

I shrugged. It made no difference either way. It

was possible to be dispassionate about her, although I sensed a growing respect between us that could be the basis of a friendship of equals.

But also, however much I wanted to rationalize it, I had to acknowledge a physical component — I was fascinated by her mouth. Firm, full lips, with a slight upward curl at the corners.

What would it be like to kiss her ...

Don't even think about it. She's completely open about being a lesbian, and if you make a move on her, you'll be outed, Alex. Why should she keep your secrets?

I frowned. I certainly couldn't afford — and didn't want — a fling with Lee, presuming it was even a possibility. What, then, did I want from her? Respect. An appreciation of myself as a person. To be accepted as an equal — not inferior, not superior, but just as myself.

CHAPTER SIX

I had been involved for the past six months in the organization of the Tern Island convention. The Australasian tourist industry, through A.P.P., had enticed tour wholesalers from all over the world with one purpose in mind — to make them aware of the range of products that our ground operators had developed to service in-bound tourists. We might well have one of the most spectacular continents on earth, but it was useless just to point out a sensational waterfall, an awe-inspiring gorge, or unique and fascinating wildlife; wholesalers wanted exhaustive details regarding which local tours covered the best "must see" locations that suited their particular niche markets.

Some wholesalers sampled a selection of tours and then were happy to let us act as their agent and mix and match for them. Others, like Lee Paynter, had a hands-on approach and insisted on experiencing most of the individual tours themselves. The first days of the convention were designed to allow the delegates to sample first-hand some of the beauties of Queensland and to relax in the luxury Tern Island had to offer. At the end of this week, however, as a climax to the convention, A.P.P. was presenting the equivalent of a trade fair, where the very best of Australian and New Zealand ground content would be shown. So far everything seemed to be going to plan, but I was nervous about the success of the second half — it was make or break time.

I spent the next day attending to last minute details of the exhibitions and checking through the package for Lee that had been expressed from Sydney. Our head office was efficient, not only providing all the information I'd requested, but presenting it in an elegant customized pastel-blue briefcase. The comprehensive documentation included a synopsis of each tour, with timetables, maps, graphs, illustrations and cost structures detailing the range of options.

In the late afternoon Sir Frederick came striding into the administration block. He was in high good humor, rubbing his hands together and smiling. "Excellent cruise, Alexandra, excellent. Did you know Tony was an amateur astronomer? He brought a small telescope with him — built it himself, he said. Last night we all took turns to look at the heavens." He shook his head. "The night sky's glorious, I can't imagine why we didn't think of doing this before. I'm going to suggest the *Ocean Dream* have someone well-versed in astronomy for future cruises, since it was such a success."

Jackie Luff bustled up with messages and reminders, but he waved her away. "Later, Jackie. Could you arrange for a pot of coffee and something to eat? Alexandra and I will be in my office."

Jackie directed a malevolent look in my direction. I was beginning to suspect that it was the attention Sir Frederick paid to me that was the problem, although I couldn't decide if Jackie's dislike was motivated by jealousy or just sheer bloody-mindedness.

Sir Frederick was full of hearty goodwill. "Sit down, sit down! I see we have the information for Lee Paynter. Let's go through it, shall we? You're pleased with it?"

I was tired and irritable and had already checked every detail, but of course I was politely agreeable, even when Sir Frederick brought his chair around my side of the desk and sat knee to knee with me. I moved my chair until there was a reasonable distance between us. He flipped through the sections, commenting now and then, but it seemed to me it was an excuse to keep me there. I was pleased when we were interrupted by Jackie's entry with a tray of refreshments, because it gave me an opportunity to stand up and do a coffee-pouring, what-will-you-have-to-eat routine.

I sighed to myself when Sir Frederick made it

clear we were to resume our former proximity. He sipped his coffee, then said warmly, "I'm very pleased with the job you're doing. You've already demonstrated your organizational skills, but dealing with someone like Lee Paynter's another matter. She's made it perfectly clear to me that she's impressed by you." He leaned forward to pat my hand. "That's excellent. Excellent."

The hand-patting sealed it. I moved my hand from under his as obviously as possible, and he certainly noticed the gesture, although he seemed not the slightest abashed. Inwardly I groaned. Steve was right, blast him. Sir Frederick's interest in me was not wholly professional — in fact, looking at his warmly approving expression, it clearly wasn't professional at all.

I cursed silently. This was a complication I didn't need. I resented the fact that I'd have to spend time working out a strategy to achieve the difficult task of discouraging Sir Frederick and not compromising my job at the same time.

Fearing that any moment he might say something we would both regret, I gulped down my coffee and hastily gathered up the material from the tour briefcase. "Would you like me to drop this off at Lee's cabana?"

"Why, yes." He was still beaming at me. "She should see it as soon as possible."

I made what I hoped was a graceful exit and walked with rising anticipation towards the beach. I wanted to see Lee again, not for any particular reason, but because she was one of those people, I had decided, whose energy flows into the space around them, so that they move in a field of electric vitality.

I wasn't prepared for the disappointment I felt when my knock went unanswered — it was ridiculous, because I knew I'd be likely to run into her later in the evening. Scribbling a brief note, I left the pastel briefcase propped up against her door and went to my own cabana to shower and change for dinner.

New Zealand and each Australian state had their own representatives promoting tourism, and every evening audio-visual presentations designed to catch the attention of even the most jaded of professional travel operators were shown during the latter stages of dinner to a captive audience. The program tonight began with the spectacular beauties of the Northern Territory. Image after image — Kakadu National Park, the MacDonnell Ranges, Ayers Rock, the Olgas, the Eqaninga rock carvings, Standley Chasm, Katherine Gorge — cascaded across the screen in combination with the timeless sounds of the clicking sticks and didgeridoos used in Aboriginal corroborees. It pleased me that the presentation ended too soon, leaving the audience hungry for more.

I had been watching for Lee and had seen her, looking a little sunburnt, come in late to dinner. Now, as coffee was served, she came over to my table. Before she could speak, I said, "You got the additional tour information? I left it at your cabana."

"I had a quick look at it. I was impressed."

Her comment embarrassed me. Perhaps she thought I was fishing for compliments because I'd been responsible for putting the package together. I know I sounded abrupt as I changed the subject with, "How was the cruise?"

"Great. Can I buy you a drink? I'd like to go over some details about tomorrow's tour with you."

Inwardly reluctant because I was feeling brittle and on edge, I nevertheless agreed. I walked with her silently, thinking how much I disliked the lounge bar, not only because of its noisy, almost frantic, conviviality, but also because its pseudo-tropical decor grated. I could stand just so much split bamboo, plaited curtains and garish artificial tropical flowers, not to mention the archly named cocktails.

Lee obviously shared my aversion. She halted in the doorway, grimaced at the cacophony, then suggested we go outside by the floodlit pool where only a few of the white tables were occupied. I knew that my well-schooled expression showed none of the tension I felt, and the bottle of French champagne she ordered I welcomed as something to abate my anxiety.

Lee raised her glass in a toast. "To the next weeks. Let's enjoy them."

She wanted additional details about her itinerary for the following few days and I answered succinctly. I hoped to make it an early night, but courtesy made me ask perfunctory questions about the overnight cruise. Lee seemed happy to talk for hours. I hid my impatience and eventually the champagne relaxed me to the point where I was chatting with superficial animation, although with little concentration.

"Alex?"

I was jerked to attention. "Sorry, I didn't catch what you said."

"We've finished one bottle of champagne between us. Do you want another?"

"No, thanks. Actually I might call it a night. I'm tired."

Lee stood. "I'll walk with you."

We left the goodtime noise of the bar for a perfect tropical night, so perfect it was a cliche. A huge yellow moon sailed serenely in a velvet sky, a soft breeze blew exotic scents from the shadowed gardens, and coconut fronds whispered overhead. We stopped at the edge of the sand to gaze out at the silvered water sighing onto the pale sand.

"This is too good to be true," I said. "It's rather like being on a film set."

Lee's smile shone white in the moonlight. "What part are you playing?"

"Myself."

Lee laughed softly. "You're such a woman of mystery, Alex, I don't know who that is."

Disconcerted by the warm intimacy of her tone, I turned and began to walk along the upper side of the beach, passing in and out of the black serrated shadows of the palm leaves. Lee paced with me, silent.

We might have been alone on a deserted island: the noise from the bar had faded, to be replaced by the ripple of water running gently up the sand and the faint rustle of leaves as the warm perfumed air moved gently under the silver light.

Lee's cabana was next to mine. I stopped at the short path that led to it. Low subtle lighting made the path discernible, but did not dispel the darkness under the trees. "Well, goodnight . . ."

"So soon?" she said. She sounded amused. "And on such a romantic evening?"

As we stood facing each other I was silent, mesmerized by the moonlight, by the soft air, by her physical proximity. She took my hand. The contact was enough to compel me to take that one step into her arms.

I could smell her light perfume, feel the taut muscles in her back, hear a murmur deep in her throat. We kissed gently, carefully . . . But then Lee's mouth opened beneath mine, her tongue flickered along my lips, her arms tightened about me.

I wanted to draw back. Lee was making demands I couldn't, wouldn't meet. I heard myself groan. It wasn't enough. Part of me wanted more, more. Lee's lips had shocked me into an electric craving. Involuntarily I opened my mouth fully to her insistent tongue.

Drowning in sensation, I struggled to assert some control. *Be careful, you'll melt, you'll be lost.*

It was easier when I held Lee at arms' length. "I'm sorry. I didn't mean . . . Forget it happened."

"Forget?" Lee's voice had a faint tremor that was both exciting and frightening. "I doubt that I'll forget."

Conscious that Lee hadn't moved, I made myself walk at a controlled pace to the refuge of my cabana. Closing the door behind me, I stood in the cocoon of darkness. How could I have been so unbelievably stupid, so determined to stall my career? I snapped on the light. Agitated and angry, I began to move aimlessly about the room. I could clearly hear my mother's words, a well-worn phrase so often repeated: "If you play with fire, you'll get burned." My family had a store of such sayings, most of them concerned with the results of careless, immoral or foolish behavior.

What had I done? For a moment's gratification, for an impulse I'd made no attempt to control ...

I went into the bathroom and examined myself in the mirror. I was pale, the contrast of my black hair and dark eyes more emphatic, but my face was familiar in its composure. I watched my lips turn up in a humorless smile.

Okay, Alex, let's see you get out of this.

CHAPTER SEVEN

It was to be a very early start the next morning, so my alarm jarred me awake when birds were greeting the sun with almost indecent enthusiasm. The day's program included a helicopter ride to Port Douglas, a sumptuous tropical breakfast at a luxurious hotel, a flight over the Reef which ran closest to the mainland at that point, and then sightseeing in the Cape Tribulation World Heritage Rainforest. I lay staring at the ceiling, reluctant to make the first move in what promised to be, at the very least, a trying day — Lee was to be one of the four who were my responsibility.

I was light-headed with fatigue. When I'd at last dozed off, my sleep had been broken by restless dreams and half-awake imaginings as I played the scene over and over. What would the consequences be? What would Lee do? What should *I* do?

Of one thing I was sure: if I was to have any hope of salvaging my self-respect and putting our relationship back on a professional footing, I'd have to speak to Lee immediately, not let the situation slide into mutual awkwardness.

Shocked fully awake by a cold shower, I dressed with care in crisp lemon pants and a top edged with a slightly deeper yellow pattern. Surveying the results in a full-length mirror, I thought ruefully that the yellow was not only a pleasing foil for my dark hair, but it also effectively emphasized the blue-black circles under my eyes.

Gathering my resolution, I took one last look at my self-possessed expression, and walked quickly over to Lee's cabana. Not allowing myself to hesitate, I knocked sharply.

She opened the door immediately. She looked rested, secure. There was a moment's pause before she said casually, "Hi. I'm almost ready."

"I'd like to say something . . ."

She smiled slightly, made an open-handed gesture. "There's no need."

I took a deep breath. "There is. Last night . . . I was stupid, out of line. I want you to know it won't happen again."

"That would be a pity."

Her light tone generated instant anger. "Don't

play with me! I'm embarrassed enough as it is, without you taking cheap shots."

Lee, obviously surprised at my vehemence, said, "Alex, I'm sorry. I didn't mean you to take it that way."

In control again, I managed to sound almost offhand as I offered, "I'd like to forget it. Never mention it again. Okay?"

She regarded me thoughtfully. "If that's what you want, of course. As far as I'm concerned it never happened."

The helicopter flight to Port Douglas and the elaborate tropical breakfast laid out at the luxury hotel passed in a haze of disconnected images, although I must have behaved appropriately, as no one gazed at me in consternation or amusement. Otto, whom I was beginning to regard affectionately as "my German" asked his usual involved questions and then listened to my answers as though studying for an examination; Mr. Moto, a rather chubby, reticent Japanese gentleman, recorded everything on his complicated video camera; Hilary Ferguson, her wide blue eyes hidden by outsize dark glasses, said little but looked fetchingly demure in pale pink; and Lee — Lee laughed, moved, spoke with brash energy, as though nothing had occurred between us.

Several strong cups of coffee during breakfast had nudged me back into some semblance of normality and as our helicopter pilot checked the instruments, I withdrew from the general conversation to consider the situation. I was relieved by Lee's assurances that she'd forget anything had happened. And, after all, what was it but a slip of judgment that led to one too-intimate moment? It wasn't as if we'd made love ...

She had taken the seat beside the pilot and was in the middle of an animated conversation about the range of tourist flights offered in Northern Queensland. Dismayingly, not only could I recreate with tantalizing vividness the taste of her mouth and my body's responses, but my unruly thoughts went further, leaping to richer, wilder imaginings.

Oh, great. A touch of overwhelming lust is just what's needed when you have to spend the next two weeks with the woman.

The helicopter lifted off with insect-like facility and banked over Port Douglas, the once sleepy coastal town that had exploded in tourist development as it capitalized on its proximity to unspoiled beaches, the Great Barrier Reef and almost untouched tropical rainforest.

As we swooped over a pattern of reefs close to the coastline, I viewed them with delight. Although from the air their huge dark shadows didn't suggest any of the beauty that underwater exploration revealed, their extent overwhelmed me. It had taken millions of years to create these gigantic fortifications against the Pacific Ocean. Feeling impelled to share some of the wonder I felt, I raised my voice above the helicopter's metallic hum. "There are two and a half thousand individual reefs and islands, stretching two thousand kilometers along the Queensland coast." I remembered to add an American perspective. "And they cover an area about half the size of Texas."

Lee grinned. "I find that downright impressive."

The helicopter banked, turning towards the beckoning green of the lush coastal vegetation. As we flew over the deeper, darker green of the rainforest canopy, it seemed to me that we were crass intruders whose tenure was brief when measured against time and the patient persistence of nature.

Our four-wheel drive vehicle was waiting, a glistening red Toyota with an incongruous showroom shine. I'd met Vince, our driver, before. "Alex!" he exclaimed, as though I were a long-lost relative. He was middle-aged and leathery, a garrulous no-nonsense bushie who had a cheerful scorn for the city and an undisguised love of the land. As clean and tidy as his vehicle, he wore a neatly pressed khaki shirt and shorts, heavy brown boots polished to a rich shine, and a brown Akubra hat tilted jauntily forward so his grinning face peered out from beneath its brim. He was the genuine article, and I thought how pseudo Steve Monahan would look beside him.

He introduced himself to everyone in turn, pumping each hand. "What's your name, mate? Otto? G'day, Otto! And? Hilary! ... Lee!"

Mr. Moto looked alarmed when his hand was seized, but eventually whispered his name. Vince seemed to see this as a victory. "So, Toshi, is it? Eh? No point in being shy, mate."

After obligingly posing with the four-wheel drive for Mr. Moto's videotape camera, Vince loaded us into the vehicle. "Okay, Alex, you've seen this all before, so in the back, eh? And Toshi, you'll want to film, so you get a window seat." He beamed at

Hilary and Lee. "I'll take you ladies up the front with me, so Otto goes in the back, too."

As we bumped along the road, Vince gestured at the overhanging vegetation. "Ever wonder why it's called a rainforest? Give you a clue. Sometimes it rains thirty-two inches in twenty-four hours." He turned to survey those of us seated behind him and I repressed the impulse to lean over and grab the steering wheel. "Four meters — say thirteen feet of rain a year ... *that's* why it's called a rainforest." He turned back to the road, jerking the wheel as we veered towards the edge. "When we get to the Daintree River, I'm going to ask you not to swim — we're particular here about what the crocs eat."

I hid my smile. The dry bush humor didn't always translate into other cultures. Mr. Moto, for example, was clearly puzzled. "Crocs? he said.

"There are crocodiles in the water," I explained.

"Big ones," said Vince, letting go the wheel to stretch his arms out wide. "Twenty, thirty feet!"

Hilary looked suitably startled. "Heavens, Vince, are they maneaters?"

Vince grinned wickedly. "Have your leg off in half a minute — less, even." He paused for effect. "What the crocs do, see, is grab you and pull you into the water. They thrash round till you drown, and then they wedge your body under a log for later. They're cunning bastards and they can move like lightning if they want to."

I said briskly, "We probably won't even see a crocodile."

We didn't. The Daintree River vehicle ferry took us across opaque army-green water apparently innocent of hazardous reptiles, although this didn't stop Hilary from peering hopefully into the murky depths.

In Vince's enthusiastic care, we ricocheted off the Daintree ferry and bounced onto the unsealed road that led to Cape Tribulation.

The canopy of the rainforest formed a ceiling so thick that we seemed to be moving through a gigantic green cave filled with hot, moist air. Great buttressed tree trunks loomed, their trunks decorated with coiling lianas, tree orchids, lichen and mosses.

"Up there," said Vince, pointing through the roof of the Toyota, "the rainforest is like a roof garden. Ferns and orchids and strangler figs — I'll show you how the strangler works when we stop — and birdwing butterflies eight inches across. That's where the ringtail possums and little sugar gliders live, but they only come out at night and they never come down to the ground."

The Toyota growled as the incline became steeper. To our right the land dropped away in a slope so steep that the tree trunks seemed to be hugging the earth as they struggled to reach the light. Mr. Moto's camera whirred as he filmed the precipitous fall; Otto, after one horrified look, squashed me by leaning hard to his left, obviously working on the theory that his considerable weight would provide a counterbalance should we teeter on the edge.

This amused Lee. She turned around to smile at him. "We wouldn't go far, Otto. The trees would stop us."

Suddenly, dazzlingly, there was a break in the canopy. We all blinked in the glare as Vince jerked the four-wheel drive to a halt at the top of the incline. "This place's called the Window because you can look out and see the world outside the rainforest. See, back there ... that's where we've come from. There's the Daintree emptying into the sea."

To me the lush vegetation seemed to seethe in a relentless struggle for existence. Trees, vines, ferns, palms, scrabbled for space and light. Insects hummed, the moisture rose like a palpable mist, the very earth seemed voluptuously alive. Far below us was a narrow coastal plain and then the brilliant aquamarine of the Coral Sea, blurring where the green snake of the Daintree River blended with it.

Otto exclaimed as a huge butterfly, a flash of brilliant electric blue, dipped and swerved in the sunlight. "That's a Ulysses," said Vince. "Watch it when it settles. It'll disappear."

Like a living sapphire, the Ulysses glided, banked, floated — as though deliberately displaying its beauty — then sank down towards a blossom, closed its wings and became virtually invisible as the dull brown underside blended with the background.

A small bird with a curved bill and a deep yellow breast darted into the clearing. "The butterfly!" said Hilary.

Vince patted her arm. "Relax. It's a sunbird. Eats nectar, not insects. That's a female, and she's pretty, but wait till you see her mate."

The little bird gave a high-pitched hissing whistle, and as if on cue another sunbird appeared. His wings and back were olive, and part of his front was yellow, but he had a bib of a brilliant metallic purplish-blue. Joining the female at a bush covered in red blossoms, hovering with beating wings, he plunged his beak into a flower.

I looked at Lee. She was watching the birds, a smile lighting her face. My body reminded me I'd kissed her last night; my mind issued a sharp warning.

We started off again, reentering the closed, shaded environment of the rainforest. Vince was filled with proprietorial pleasure as he parked the Toyota beside a sign announcing the Marrdja walk. "Right!" he said, waving his arms until we formed an obedient group in front of him. "Marrdja means rainforest in the local Aboriginal language, in case you were going to ask. Keep to the boardwalk and don't go tramping round off the track."

The forest floor was patterned with moving patches of light as the sun searchlighted through breaks in the roof of vegetation. "Look up there," said Vince, pointing. I was amused to see how we all followed his instructions, tilting our heads to gaze at the huge palms with fronds shaped like open, fringed umbrellas. "Those are rare Fan Palms — only found in this area."

After we'd spent the required time in admiration, he set off again, explaining why the floor of the rainforest, apart from succulent plants and ferns, was so surprisingly clear. "Leaves, twigs, branches — they're falling all the time, and in this climate the layers just rot away and turn themselves into soil. Most plants need more than the dim light you get here at ground level. When a rainforest tree falls and the sun shines in through the break in the canopy, things spring up and fight for the light —

and the ones that win block the hole with their foliage, so the losers die."

With the toe of his boot he disturbed the surface near a rotting log, uncovering a huge and indignant cricket. "A king cricket," he said to Hilary, who had drawn back with a muttered exclamation. "And if you think *it's* big, you should see the cockroaches we get here — you could throw a saddle over them!"

Lee stopped by a gigantic tree, its trunk a massive tangle of thick root-like protrusions that formed an elaborate criss-cross pattern. "What's this? It looks as if its trunk's been braided."

Vince patted the tree affectionately. "Strangler fig," he said. "Told you I'd give you the info on this one. It starts off when the fruit is eaten by flying foxes or birds, and the seeds drop into the canopy up above us. The fig seed starts to grow in the angle of a branch or in a little hollow — and mind, this is ninety, maybe a hundred feet in the air. And then it begins to send long, thin roots down to the floor where we are, making a curtain around the poor bastard of a tree it's growing on. And when they reach the earth, whacko! Its roots get fatter and stronger and begin to strangle its host, while its leaves at the top screen out the sun, so the other tree dies. And then it's won."

Vince pointed to skeins of thin vines. "And these are climbing palms or rattans. They never get any fatter, see, and some are hundreds of feet long. They climb using hooks to hang on with." He grinned. "In Australia we call them lawyer vines, because once the buggers get their hooks into you, they never let you go."

Lee left us to go striding off along the wooden

walkway. Suddenly she stopped, then leaned over. She turned back to us, gesturing us to be quiet. I smiled when I saw the echidna, or spiny anteater. It was shoving its long snout into the layers of leaves on the rainforest floor, now and then pausing to rake at the vegetable matter with its impressive claws.

In a whisper, Vince said, "Suppose the echidna looks like a hedgehog to most of you, but it's not related, even if it has got spines and eats insects. It's a unique little Aussie, along with the platypus — they both lay eggs like a bird, but they're mammals, and suckle their babies."

Our concentrated stares seemed to impinge on the echidna. It stopped snuffling in the rotting leaves, looked in our direction with tiny black eyes, then rapidly rolled itself into a prickly ball of long brown spines.

Otto ventured to touch the bristling spikes, but it only rolled itself tighter. As Mr. Moto kneeled to take his inevitable video shot, Lee said to me, "I've known people like that — cute, but they only let you see the prickles."

I nodded, wanting to say, "Do you mean me?" — but unwilling to run the risk that she'd look at me blankly and say, "You?"

In the distance there was the long drawn out ringing crack of the male whipbird followed by the female's answering "choo choo" sound. Vince beckoned to us. "Take a look at this."

He beamed at us. "Leaf-tailed gecko. Lurks around, looking like a piece of bark — see how its sides are sort of fringed, so it won't throw a definite shadow — till some unwary insect, or smaller lizard, or even a green tree frog, chances by and becomes lunch."

I've always had a soft spot for green tree frogs. Apart from their brilliant color, they have suckers on their feet and can climb expanses of glass, reminding me of mountaineers gingerly traversing a cliff-face. They also, I'm convinced, have a keen sense of humor. I remembered one incident that must have caused great frog amusement. I'd been escorting a very fastidious Swiss tour operator around Queensland and at one overnight stop at Cape York he had visited the rather primitive bathroom facilities. Rushing back to me with horrified indignation, insisting that I accompany him, he complained that a bright green frog had been grinning at him from beneath the rim of the toilet bowl.

"Do they swim in the cistern?" he had demanded.

"Watch," I'd said as I flushed the toilet. In the swirl of water two green bodies catapulted from their hiding place. I could almost hear them screaming, "Whee!" as they rode the cascade. When it was still, one had disappeared through the S-bend and the other was cheerfully clambering up the smooth porcelain. I was delighted by their feats — the Swiss gentleman had been far less impressed.

"What are you smiling at?" said Lee.

"Tree frogs. I'll tell you later."

Vince was waxing lyrical: "If I had you here at night, we'd go spotlighting, and you'd see wallabies, and tree kangaroos, and flying foxes, and little marsupial potoroos about the size of rabbit, and cuscusses with round heads, no ears and great big staring eyes ..."

* * * * *

We drove on towards the coast and Cape
Tribulation, Vince still buoyant with enthusiasm.
"Want to know why it's called Cape Tribulation?" It
was a rhetorical question. He went on before anyone
could respond, "Seventeen-seventy it was, and
Captain Cook who was in the middle of discovering
Australia, hit a reef just off this headland. The
Endeavour didn't sink, but the whole thing caused
him so much trouble he called the place Cape
Tribulation." He shook his head. "Sailing round the
world in those little wooden boats — that took real
guts."

We stopped at a beach where we were to have
lunch at the luxury resort nestled in the rainforest.
Vince leaped out of the Toyota and made a grand,
encompassing gesture. "Reef, rainforest and beach!"

The lush vegetation balked at the edge of the
pink-beige sand, which, deserted, stretched towards a
distant headland. Green water washed in lazy
ripples, and overhead the arch of the sky held so
deep a blueness it seemed to vibrate.

I was tired, both emotionally and physically. The
sunlight was too bright, the beauty too
overwhelming. Suddenly I felt the weight of time
pressing upon me — the realization that the
landscape had looked very like this for at least a
million years. Bizarre creatures — gigantic
kangaroos, rhinoceros-sized wombats, huge ferocious
marsupials — had roamed in primeval forests
crowding the shore as the rainforest did now; the
sea had teemed with monstrous creations while tiny

coral polyps were beginning the foundations of the bulwarks that would become the Great Barrier Reef.

I started when Lee spoke close beside me, her words echoing my thoughts. "This is such an ancient continent."

Vince overheard her. "The oldest in the world," he said proudly. "We've got rocks in the Outback scientists can date to three thousand million years."

Otto, whose passion was for information, wanted to know more details. Mr. Moto had lost interest as there was nothing to videotape. Hilary smiled winningly as she said, "Lunch, Vince? I'm starving."

The meal was a success, with fresh seafood served simply, to enhance its flavor, but I did not taste what I ate. Vince was to drive us back to the helicopter so we could fly down the spectacular coastline between Port Douglas and Cairns. Fatigue had almost swamped me, and I sat mute in the middle of the back seat, with Otto's bulk on one side and Mr. Moto and his ubiquitous video camera on the other. Hilary and Lee were deep in conversation and I felt a twinge of ... jealousy? I closed my eyes, deciding I was too tired to think straight ...

I could almost smile — *straight* wasn't what I was thinking at all.

The eggbeater chatter of the helicopter was an irritation, and I barely glanced at the magnificent beaches — secluded stretches of sand lapped by a jewel sea, fringed with palms — that ran in a continuous stream beneath us. I wished that Vince had come too. He would know every headland, every beach, plus some unique point or story for each.

But perhaps we'd all had a surfeit of beauty. Mr. Moto had stopped videotaping, Otto gazed mutely out the window, Hilary covered a yawn with a graceful hand. Lee was sitting beside the pilot, but, for once, she had no questions. I examined her incisive features in profile. She looked strong, determined, implacable. I was sure she'd keep her word. She'd act as though there had been no kiss, no indiscretion on my part. But would she forget it? *I* couldn't.

CHAPTER EIGHT

I went to bed tired and melancholy. I awoke refreshed and melancholy. As I stretched and yawned, wisps of dreams floated in my mind, twisting and dissolving in the light. Had I dreamed of Lee? I had a memory of her low chuckle fading as the clock radio came alive with a blare of music.

Leaping out of bed was the last thing I wanted to do. I killed the radio, then burrowed back into the sheets and hid my face in the pillow. Half-dozing, my traitorous imagination filled me with sweet erotic sensations. Kissing Lee again — the texture of her mouth, the pressure of her body against mine making me gasp . . .

I sat up.

This is bloody hopeless. I'm infatuated with a woman who would laugh if she knew what I was feeling. I've got to preserve some dignity, not to mention preserving my career . . .

Remembering that an early staff meeting was scheduled, I got out of bed in a mini-rage. I encouraged my anger — it was a means of countering the desire that disturbed and confused me because it wasn't just a physical imperative, and I was absolutely determined to ignore any deeper dimension. I'd been well-taught not to hope for too much because disappointment was all the keener, then.

Have some pride, Alex. She can't reject you if you stay aloof.

I could lecture myself as much as I liked. My imagination escaped my will and skittered away to build enticing images. Lee was a lesbian. She loved women. She showed she enjoyed my company. She'd opened her mouth and kissed me, really kissed me. And if I'd stayed, not run away, what would have happened?

I headed for the bathroom. "Cold shower," I prescribed aloud, savage with myself. A kiss was just a kiss. Making love was several magnitudes greater than a casual embrace. Lee was a professional . . . for God's sake, *I* was a professional. And Sharon had said Lee didn't mix business with pleasure. There was no reason for me to suppose she'd break her rules for Alex Findlay.

I could even manage a rueful smile. *Pity ... but there it is.*

Today was vital to the success of the convention. Our home-grown Aussie tour operators would exhibit their wares to the hard-eyed evaluation of international wholesalers as well as small niche companies who dealt in specialist group tours. This was the day when package deals were constructed, contracts drafted, tourism potential realized.

The purpose of the early staff meeting was to pump us up to maximum efficiency and enthusiasm. We were all required to dress in white, our identification badges prominently displayed. We all had specific jobs, and mine was "enabler/facilitator" — Sir Frederick had lately taken to employing jargon plucked from psychology and management theory — my function being to make sure that negotiations between ground operators and wholesalers went smoothly and that all details were taken care of as unobtrusively and efficiently as possible. My special responsibilities were Lee Paynter and Otto Schmidt, although all A.P.P. employees were expected to assist in the selling of Australian tourism in general.

I was almost late for the meeting. Fortunately Sharon's red hair stood out like a beacon, so I weaved my way through the crowd to grab her arm. She was returning to Sydney the next day, and I wanted her advice before she left. "Can I have a quick word with you afterwards? It's important."

She raised a quizzical eyebrow. "Steve again?"

"No, worse luck. I know how to handle *him*."

"Sir Frederick, then."

"You've noticed?"

Sharon gave a sympathetic smile. "That, and a little vicious gossip from Jackie Luff. I was going to tell you about it after the meeting. She's spreading the word that you're sleeping your way to the top."

"Oh, great!"

Sir Frederick tapped the lectern for attention. Jackie Luff, playing loyal lieutenant, glared for silence. I glared back at her. "I don't need this on top of everything else," I said to Sharon. "I'm going to sort her out."

She grinned widely. "Can I watch? Jackie's had it coming for a long time."

Sir Frederick rapped the lectern with obvious impatience. Silence fell, he let it stretch for a moment, then began. "I hardly need to say how important today is, for now we reap the rewards for all our work over the past months ..."

Keeping an attentive expression on my face, I tuned out his clipped British voice and tried to evaluate what I was feeling. It often helps me get a clear picture if I select words to describe my reactions to a situation. Sitting in the meeting, my unfocused gaze fixed on Sir Frederick's dapper figure, I came up with *jangled, uptight, combative* and, sneaking in under my guard, *infatuated*. I smiled wryly. Lee Paynter's power to disturb my equanimity was extraordinary.

The meeting ended and Sharon and I walked out into the sunlight. Steve came up to us, handsome in crisp white and wearing a triumphant smile. I reflected that he always looked smug, as though he'd recently checked in a mirror and been well pleased with what he saw.

"Was I right, or was I right?" he said to me, with a covert gesture towards Sir Frederick.

I had a satisfying mental picture of jabbing two fingers into his eyes as I said cheerfully, "Hope you're not relying on Jackie for your information. She's got the wrong end of the stick."

As I spoke, Sir Frederick's personal assistant emerged from the meeting room. I left Sharon and Steve and stood in front of her. "Jackie, I want to speak with you. Now. And in private."

She tried to step around me. "I'm too busy —"

"Right now, Jackie. It won't take long."

I had my fury well leashed, but some of it colored my voice. Jackie, red-faced, acquiesced. We went back into the empty meeting room and I closed the door behind us. I didn't raise my voice; my mother had taught me well how effective a soft, biting tone can be. "I've been told that you're spreading rumors about me and Sir Frederick."

Jackie wouldn't look at me directly. She shrugged, pouted, said resentfully, "Don't know what you mean."

"I understand you've told several people I have a sexual relationship with Sir Frederick."

She blinked at my bluntness. "Who told you that?"

I wasn't going to be sidetracked into who said what to whom. "Do you really want to bring other people into this? It's ugly enough as it is, but if necessary, I'm prepared to go right to the top. My reputation's important to me, both professionally and personally, and there's no truth whatsoever in this gossip."

She glowered at me. "You don't care that he's lonely. It's just a chance for you to get on, to take advantage. Sir Frederick's lost his wife and his family's grown up, so he's an easy mark, isn't he?"

Exasperated, I said, "That's ridiculous. You have no right to spread a story you know is untrue. And you'll bear the consequences."

Silence. Jackie shifted uneasily. My mention of going right to the top was an unambiguous threat, and she knew the outcome would be damaging. Finally she said, "So what do you want *me* to do about it?"

"You're going to stop repeating this story right now. You're going to deny it's true if anyone mentions it to you again." My anger began to bubble over. I spoke with greater vehemence. "Basically, Jackie, you're going to shut up!"

I didn't want to let her save face. I didn't want to end our conversation with any hint of reconciliation. As she opened the door I said, "And don't do it again."

It was a victory of sorts. Sharon would hose down any murmurings on the grapevine and the gossip, unless repeated, would grow cold quickly and be displaced by the latest hot rumor, so I didn't see the need to personally contradict what Jackie had said. Time would take care of that for me.

But what if the rumor had linked me with Lee? What if Jackie had been spreading gossip that I was a lesbian? I couldn't cope with that ... not now — not ever.

* * * * *

By evening, Sir Frederick had pronounced the day a resounding success. It had passed quickly for me as I shuttled between Otto and Lee, although both of them had done their homework, knew what they wanted and therefore only needed me to locate specific people and accomplish introductions.

Many of the delegates would be leaving Tern Island the next day, some going on to destinations within Australia accompanied by A.P.P. personnel, others to return home. For this reason the evening dinner was an official farewell, although a low-key one. I dressed with special care in high waisted silk pants and matching full-sleeved top of a golden amber shade which emphasized the darkness of my hair and eyes.

I was seated at the official table and I found myself watching for Lee. She walked in with Hilary, who was wearing an outrageously low-cut outfit in shocking pink that, of course, looked wonderful on her. Lee, in contrast, wore a light blue dress of a color so pale it was almost white. She also had on the silver mesh bracelet of the first night. She smiled at me as she took her seat.

After dinner, Sir Frederick's speech was graceful and brief, and then he asked a small group of us to join him for coffee in his cabin. He led the way with Mr. Wen from Korea, Sir Frederick taking large strides that forced the much shorter man to almost trot to keep up. I walked in companionable silence with Tony and Sharon through the provocative caress of the warm heavy-scented air. Behind us

Hilary Ferguson was laughing with Lee over some story. Unwillingly I considered how much time they seemed to now spend together ...

More opulently furnished than the cabanas, the cabins were designed for entertaining. Sir Frederick's luxurious accommodation was hidden behind screens of judiciously positioned flowering bushes, to give the impression that the cabin was situated in its own lush garden, far from any other building. The main room had deep lounges, a thick white carpet and French windows opening onto a stone patio. A waiter stood ready to serve us coffee and a selection of tiny cakes while Sir Frederick bonhomied around the room with a tray of liqueurs. I accepted a black coffee. Having had wine with dinner, I was wary of combining proximity to Lee with more alcohol.

I circled the room, chatting for a few moments to each person, spending more time with Otto, who gallantly declared he was heartbroken to be leaving me. I didn't speak to Lee. Eventually I ran into Tony, who was taking a similar circular route, but in the opposite direction. "We've done our duty," he said. "Let's find somewhere to relax."

Tony sank down beside me on an ample russet couch. "I like substantial furniture, Alex. It matches my substantial self." There was a burst of laughter from the other side of the room where Hilary, obviously in a sparkling mood, was entertaining Lee and Steve, although it seemed obvious to me that she was concentrating on Lee. The laughter made Tony smile too. He looked approvingly at Hilary, saying, "She's quite beautiful, isn't she?"

His tone was appreciative, but there was no

sexual connotation at all. Not for the first time, I wondered about Tony. He'd been married and had children, but his divorce had gone through years ago and his kids were almost grown up.

He nudged me gently. "Take a look at Steve over there." The conversation between Lee and Hilary was an animated one, and Steve's obvious attempts to take over were being thwarted. Tony said with marked irony, "Could Steve be getting the cold shoulder? Surely no one would deny him the center of attention?"

"It seems that way," I said lightly. Deliberately turning my attention to Tony, I tried to ignore the two women, but I felt a stab of ... what? Resentment? Jealousy?

It helped me when Sir Frederick pulled up a chair and joined us. He was delighted with the achievements of the day and wanted our perceptions of its success, so I could concentrate on answering his questions and giving my evaluations. And tonight his attitude towards me was his customary business-like formality. It was tempting to think he'd heard the rumor Jackie had been circulating and had decided to retreat.

When several others engaged Sir Frederick's attention I took the opportunity to escape. The room was full of noise — laughter, conversation, the clink of cups and glasses. As the familiar feeling of alienation swamped me, I made my way unobtrusively to the French windows and slipped outside. A few paces into the garden reduced the voices to background noise. I sat on a stone bench to let the peace of the night soak into me. The rising moon spilled black and white, crickets — no doubt of giant size — were calling and the scent of tropical flowers vitalized the light breeze.

"May I join you?" said Lee.

My heart leapt — not with surprise, nor joy — but with fear. It was not because I desired her with a passion whose carnal force bewildered me; I could contend with that. But what I felt for Lee ... it had another dimension, a deeper, darker, more dangerous measure.

"Alex?"

Would her voice always be a blow to the heart?

"Yes?"

She stood gazing at me, frowning. "Is something the matter?"

I looked away. "Yes ..."

Say it. For once dare to say what you think and feel.

The moonlight poured into the garden, the crickets sang. I looked up at her. "I want to go to bed with you."

Lee's lips began to curve in a smile. "Let's do it."

"Just like that?"

Her husky chuckle caught my breath. "Just like that."

We didn't speak, didn't touch, as we walked the moonlit paths to Lee's cabana. I was disconnected, fatalistic. Whatever happened — happened. And if was a failure, if I made a total fool of myself — then that was how it had to be.

Lee put the key in the door, opened it, gestured me inside. She looked calm, concentrated, remote.

She's done this a thousand times before. It's no big deal for her.

The room was dim, the only illumination a lamp beside the bed. I could hear the blood beating in my ears. Lee was standing, waiting.

I looked into her shadowed eyes, saw her hold out her arms, walked like an automaton into her embrace.

The heat of Lee's mouth awakened a shocking, ravenous desire. I trembled with it, moaned with it.

I wanted to tear her clothes off, to have bare skin under my fingers, to taste her, consume her. But it was Lee who was undressing me, never ceasing to kiss me while her hands slid under my shirt, unhooked my bra, eased my clothing off until I was bare to the waist. Bending her head, her blonde hair tickling my throat, her hands cupping my breasts, she teased my swollen nipples with her tongue and teeth.

I heard myself gasp. I had to speak. "I can't stand up any more." Was that my voice, so hoarse with passion?

Lee murmured, "Just a little longer." Now her fingers were at my belt, deft, sure — and I was helping her, desperate to be fully naked. The ache between my legs had become so urgent I wanted to seize her hand and beg her to hurry, hurry.

Wanton, it was wanton. I could hear myself panting. All my control had dissolved. "Lee, I can't wait."

The cool touch of the sheets against my hot skin, involuntarily my hips lifting, legs parting. Lee's mouth at my breast, her cupped hand strong and sure. An ecstasy of tightness clenched within me as I arched, quivering on the edge.

I could hear Lee's voice, softly commanding.

"Come for me, Alex." And then I heard myself wailing as I contorted with the waves of release.

I don't do this. Cry out like this. Feel that my bones have dissolved and my body melted . . .

I was lying with my face nestled into her neck, a delicious lassitude filling me. I was conscious of her clothing, smooth and fine against my bare skin.

"Lee?"

She chuckled deep in her throat. "Alex?"

"I'd like to undress you . . ." *What a weak word . . . I want . . . desire . . . hunger for the touch of your skin against mine.*

She simply watched as I fumbled with the zipper, her eyes dark, her lips slightly apart, curved in a faint smile. She seemed composed, passive, but a pulse thudded in her throat. Suddenly I was desperate. I had to hold her, devour her, slake my voracious thirst for her body.

"Help me," I said, my voice thick.

She got off the bed, stood while I undressed her. Her lightly tanned skin was warm under my fingers as I took off the last of her clothes. I wanted her on top of me, I wanted my fingers inside her, I wanted . . .

"Oh, God," I heard myself say.

Eyes heavy-lidded, she was looking at my mouth. Our lips, tongues met. My arms were tight about her, clamping her against me, the whole length of her body pressed hard against mine. Sensation spiraled out from the kiss, blurring into a maelstrom of feeling so intense it was like a delicious, forbidden pain.

I intended to be slow, gentle, considerate, but I was shaking with a passion screaming for the relief her body could provide. I collapsed onto the bed, pulling her with me. She went willingly, letting me turn her so her weight was on me, her breasts full and heavy, my mouth opening to their softness. My thigh was between her legs, and she moved against me, wet as I was wet, trembling as I was trembling.

There was nothing but Lee: her tumbled tawny blonde hair, her ragged breathing, the taste of her skin, the wild rhythm of her body.

I knew that I was sobbing. I knew that — but I didn't know why.

CHAPTER NINE

The flight to Cairns would leave mid-morning, so someone would soon be coming to collect my luggage. I stood listlessly looking at the items I still had to find room for, wondering why there always seemed to be more to pack than I'd brought in the first place.

I sat down on the edge of the bed. Musing on the vagaries of packing to prove to myself that everything was normal was hardly successful. Vivid images continually slipped past my guard: moonlight,

Lee's breasts, tumbled sheets, skin slippery with sweat, the agony of desire, my tears ...

"Why are you crying?" she had said, her voice gentle.

"I don't know."

She had held me, comforted me, until my passion came welling up again, flooding me with a frantic wild appetite I'd never acknowledged before.

Then we had slept. I woke at dawn, rousing her as I tried to ease myself out of her embrace.

Half-awake, she had watched me hastily dressing. "Why are you going, Alex? Come back to bed."

I had to escape. Guilt, fear, alarm, were hammering in my head.

She smiled. "Do you kiss your lovers goodbye, or do you just run?"

"I just run."

That had been four hours ago, and I'd had time enough to consider everything. For me it was a no-win situation. Passion, once safely contained within my fantasies, now was a burning actuality — the very thought of her seared me. And beneath that physical desire there was something more. I wanted to give and receive tenderness, support, understanding.

Jesus! One night with the woman and you want everlasting love. Grow up, Alex.

The one thing in my life I'd felt secure about was my career, but even that could be threatened. I despised myself for my fears, but that didn't stop my anxiety. Lee was openly lesbian. What if someone had seen me leaving her cabana? And how would she act towards me now? Would she make it obvious that our relationship had moved into intimacy?

I needn't have worried. In the mini-bus, boarding the little plane, during the trip to Cairns, waiting in the terminal for our respective flights, Lee was exactly the same as before. There were no sideways glances, no innuendoes in her conversation, no private smiles. She was, as usual, all business.

My reaction caused me bitter amusement. On one hand I was relieved, on the other, riled. Did our passionate encounter mean so little to her?

From Cairns, Sir Frederick and Steve Monahan would be taking a small party that included Hilary Ferguson to the Top End, touring Darwin and then Kakadu National Park. I was going with Tony Englert and Mr. Wen, the Korean representative — and Lee — to the Red Centre, first to Alice Springs and then on to Ayers Rock. There the others would join us before we all went back to Sydney.

It was a mercy, I decided wryly, that Sir Frederick and Steve would be safely away from me for the few days it would take to sort myself out. A few days? I could hear my rational self giving a hollow laugh at my confidence.

At Cairns airport, Sharon, who was going straight back to Sydney, hugged me goodbye, kissed my cheek, said, "You look terrific, Alex. What've you been doing?"

Sir Frederick limited himself to a hand on my shoulder and a warm smile. "As I've said before, Alexandra, I'm very pleased with your progress. We'll have to talk about your future, soon."

Steve tore himself away from Hilary Ferguson's side long enough to say in a stage whisper, "You're on a roll, darl. Play your cards right and it's all the way to Lady Alexandra."

Tony had been standing silently beside me, and as Steve walked away I saw him watching his jaunty progress with something close to hatred.

I touched his hand. "Tony, what's Steve done to you?"

His face became blank. "Nothing."

"Oh, come on! It's obvious you dislike him intensely. He's irritating and self-centered, but not worth hating, surely."

"Steve's a proper bastard," he said quietly. "Be careful of him, Alex. He's dangerous." Glancing up at the flight indicator, he changed the subject with evident relief. "The flight to the Alice is boarding . . . I'll just collect our Mr. Wen."

Tony sat with Lee, as Sir Frederick had instructed me to take the opportunity presented by the long flight to make myself agreeable to Mr. Wen. This made good sense. Should I gain promotion to regional director for Asia, a great deal of my attention would be directed towards the burgeoning Korean market.

Mr. Wen's English was excellent. Clad in rather crumpled seersucker shorts and a loud flowered shirt, he nursed a bulging photographic carry-bag on his bare knees. I had placed him in the window seat and, as the weather was fine and virtually cloudless, we discussed the various features of the immense landscape that slowly unrolled beneath the silver wings. We were flying southwest towards the geographical center of Australia, the true Outback, also called the Red Heart or the Red Centre, a vast, semi-arid, almost unpopulated land, eerily majestic with its ancient red mountain ranges, colored rocks and sandstone gorges.

As we neared Alice Springs I told him about the Todd River Boat Regatta — a typically Australian joke because the Todd is very rarely anything but a dry river bed marked with a series of waterholes, one of which gives Alice Springs its name. The regatta is held each August, the boats have no bottoms, and the crews carry them as they run furiously along the parched watercourse.

I fell silent as the land below us became even more spectacular — the stretching desert, the MacDonnell Ranges, the meandering dry beds of ancient rivers — the face of the Aborigine's Dreamtime legends.

The Alice, as it's called, is an explosion of civilization in the middle of nowhere, and every time I come in by air it strikes me as being the antipodean Palm Springs of the Australian desert.

As the plane approached the airport, Mr. Wen turned to me, exclaiming triumphantly, *"A Town Like Alice!"* thereby showing that Nevile Shute's story, whether as a book, film or television series, still captures the imagination.

Tony and Lee were two rows ahead of us and I'd noticed they'd talked — unusually quietly for Lee — during most of the trip. Now, disembarking, they both looked preoccupied and serious. For some irrational reason this niggled at me. I caught up with Tony as he strode towards baggage collection. Keeping my voice light, I said, "What in the world did you and Lee discuss? You both look positively tragic."

"It doesn't concern you, Alex."

His reaction surprised and hurt me. I'd thought our friendship allowed me to ask such questions. "Sorry."

He stopped. "Look, I didn't mean ... it's something I can't discuss."

"You obviously can with Lee."

He nodded soberly. "Yes, I can with Lee."

There was no point in asking why; his expression indicated the matter was closed. I made a cheerful, inconsequential remark to indicate I understood the subject was off-limits while I considered his puzzling reticence. What could he discuss with Lee, a comparative stranger, that he couldn't discuss with me?

It had been a long flight and the four of us were silent in the taxi on the way to the Sheraton. Lee brightened at the sight of the golf course adjoining the hotel, and, after I'd begged off, she roped Mr. Wen and Tony into an early morning round. "We could find a tennis court later," she said to me with a grin.

"Not enough time, unless you want to wreck your schedule — and I know how precious *that* is to you."

"No sparring," said Tony with a fine imitation of Sir Frederick's pukka English accent. "I must remind you, Alexandra, that an overseas wholesaler is always right, no matter how unreasonable her demands."

Lee's smile widened as she glanced at me. It was the first hint of conspiracy between us, and I felt my face grow hot with memories of what *I* had demanded from her.

Suddenly I felt embarrassed and insecure. What

115

did she really think of me? A woman to pass a few pleasant hours with ... or something more?

The four of us ate a subdued evening meal, chatted for a while over coffee, then mutually agreed that an early night was indicated.

Lee let the other two get ahead of us, then, half-smiling, made eye contact. "Alex ...?"

Her intention was unmistakable. I shook my head. "No."

My voice sounded flat and unfriendly. She looked at me for a long moment, then nodded slightly. "See you tomorrow, then."

Alone in my room I paced the thick carpet, impatient, unhappy, irresolute. Why had I turned Lee down? I could hardly expect her to swear undying devotion on the strength of one night together ...

Don't made a big drama of it. Why not just enjoy her while she's here?

She answered on the second ring. "Lee Paynter."

"Can I change my mind?"

A low, delighted chuckle. "I'll order champagne. Don't be long."

We were on the same floor, a moment's walk down the corridor, but I lingered outside her room, again indecisive. I burned with physical desire that Lee could satisfy — but I wanted more, much more than that. And she would soon be gone.

I knocked sharply, resolutely.

Lee seemed perfectly at ease. She handed me a brimming champagne glass. "What's worrying you, Alex?"

"Worrying me?"

"There are no strings, if that's the problem ... that's not my style."

"It's just for laughs?" I suggested.

She put down her champagne, moved closer, her eyes darkening, her breathing rough. Taking my glass from me, she said, "It's for more than laughs ..."

Her mouth tasted of toothpaste and champagne. I broke the kiss, said inanely, "You've cleaned your teeth."

"Haven't you?"

I began to smile. "Yes."

"Then we're even."

Tonight, I promised myself, I'll savor our lovemaking, not allow the unrestrained urgencies of my body to engulf me.

Promises, promises. The flame swept up my stomach, danced in my fingertips, roared in my ears. "Lee, hurry, before I short-circuit!"

We undressed in a flurry of shed clothing. I pulled her down onto the plush carpet.

"Cave woman!" she gasped, half-laughing.

Lee's travel alarm jerked me awake. I opened my eyes to her blonde hair. Her back to me, I was curled so that my knees were locked behind hers, my arm around her waist. She stirred, reached out and blindly fumbled to turn off the alarm, then burrowed closer to me, clamping her arm across mine so I was trapped in her sleepy embrace.

"Lee, let me go. I shouldn't be here. And you've got an early round of golf."

"Cuddling lowers the blood pressure," she muttered.

I tugged gently to free my imprisoned arm. "If I had blood pressure any lower, I'd be dead."

"I can figure a way to put it up . . ."

"Someone might call my room."

She sighed, exasperated, and turned to face me. "So what if someone does, Alex? What if the whole goddamn world knocks at your door? So you're not there. So what?"

I sat up, crossed my arms over my naked breasts. "Look, it's easier for you . . ."

"Is that so?"

Her tone chilled me, but I blundered on. "My career's important to me and it matters what people think. I can't afford to . . ."

"Have people think you're a lesbian."

It was more comfortable to look away. "Yes."

There was a long silence. I could hear her breathing, slow and measured. At last I said, "Are you going to say anything? Tell me I'm wrong?"

"No. You make your own decisions."

Her tone indicated there was nothing more to say. I got out of the bed, found my clothes and dressed as quickly as possible. I didn't want to stay there and endure her cool regret at my cowardice. A clinging depression settled over me.

If there was any possibility that you could ever

love me, Lee, this would put a stop to it. I'm not brave like you. I'm not willing to take the risks.

Love? The word had a bitter, burning taste. I'd been right to cling to my solitary world.

I hesitated at the doorway, trying to think of something that would heal the silence between us. I said, ridiculously, "Have a good game," then stepped out into the hall, closing the door softly behind me.

The golf had obviously been a great success. Tony and Mr. Wen seemed mightily pleased with themselves when they joined me for a late breakfast. Lee was more subdued. The conversation consisted of the enthusiastic post mortem of their game that golfers seem particularly to enjoy. With masochists' delight they itemized each fluffed shot, each ball inadvertently consigned to a water hazard.

I listened for a while, then said, "There must be something wrong with me — I can't seem to see golf the way you three do. To me, it ruins a good walk."

"That's because you can't play," Tony snorted.

Lee said, "I'll teach you the finer points, Alex. Then you'll clamor to join in."

I smiled to hide my sudden misery. I wouldn't know Lee long enough to have her teach me golf, or indeed to share anything of her ordinary day-to-day life. We had a short time left in what was to her a foreign country, and then we'd go our separate ways.

Checking my watch, I reminded Lee and Mr. Wen that we had to leave shortly to see Standley Chasm, some fifty kilometers out of Alice Springs.

Tony was staying behind to check arrangements for our visit to Ayers Rock, so the three of us set out in a deluxe rental car — Sir Frederick spared no expense when good impressions were important — on a leisurely excursion to the Western MacDonnell Ranges.

It was a warm, peaceful day and I pointed out items of interest as we drove through the arid land — the grave of John Flynn, the founder of the famed Flying Doctor Service; the ghost gums, framed against the expansive backdrop of the MacDonnell Ranges, which Namatjira, one of the first Aboriginal artists to paint with Western watercolors, had translated into glowing, extraordinary paintings. A densely-packed, fast-wheeling flock of bright green budgerigars flew overhead as I parked the car and we began the ten-minute walk along a dry creek bed to Standley Chasm.

Australia uses metric measurement, as does Japan, but for Lee's sake I translated dimensions. Besides, I always think measurements in feet sound much more impressive than meters, as does Fahrenheit for temperatures. A hundred degrees seems to me a great deal hotter than its equivalent of thirty-eight Celsius.

"Standley Chasm's five meters wide — about sixteen feet — and seventy-five meters high — about two hundred and fifty feet." Mr. Wen nodded, Lee remained solemn behind her glasses.

We stopped at the entrance to the gorge. The dimensions I'd given meant nothing in isolation, but now they were translated into the most glorious of sights. So deep and narrow that the sun only shines directly into it for ten minutes just after noon, its red sides rise sheer from the rock strewn floor, the only vegetation tenacious drought-resistant shrubs that cling to cracks and crevices in the brilliantly colored walls.

We were not the only visitors; several other tourists waited with cameras at the ready for the daily illumination of the chasm. I glanced at my companions. Mr. Wen waited patiently, his camera poised. Lee stood at ease, hands in the pockets of her denim shorts, head cocked back to gaze at the deep blue strip of cloudless sky.

In my imagination I could see the earth inexorably turning, the eye of the sun ready to flood the narrow gorge with light. Then, as if caught by an incandescent searchlight, the walls flashed in brilliant shades of red, russet, ocher and gold as the earth and sun synchronized.

"Beautiful, beautiful," murmured Mr. Wen, snapping photograph after photograph.

Lee said nothing, just smiled at the radiance of the rock walls. I felt my heart turn over.

I could so easily fall in love with you ...

I spent the afternoon in Alice Springs driving Lee and Mr. Wen to various tourist attractions and to a gallery of Aboriginal art that displayed the beauty of the earth colors, the complex patterns and unique vision that presented animals in stylized X-ray form.

Wherever we went, Mr. Wen photographed everything thoroughly and Lee asked questions. We finished the day with a trip to the top of Anzac Hill at sunset to see the dying light fluoresce the vermilion MacDonnell Ranges.

Lee's manner towards me seemed exactly the same as before, but I couldn't forget the futile conversation we'd had that morning. After dinner I said I was tired, avoided her glance, and went up to my room. I *was* tired, but I also wanted to preempt further discussion. How could I explain to someone like Lee why I had to remain firmly in the closet when she was so obviously and comfortably out?

It was time to put everything in perspective. I ordered coffee from room service, sat at the table by the window and watched the lights of cars hurrying to their destinations while I considered where *I* was going.

Physically, Lee called up in me a wild response that I'd never known was there. As a person, she intrigued me. Certainly she was tough, but she could be tender, too. I thought of how she comforted me when I'd cried, another whole facet of her personality. And I remembered Sharon's evaluation that Lee had integrity. I agreed with that. I trusted her — there was none of that disturbing dissonance that so many people have, when what they say doesn't match what they do. And she was resolute: she told the world she was gay and it was someone else's problem if that wasn't acceptable.

But what did Lee think of me? She found me sexually pleasing, of that I had ample evidence. But otherwise ... We both had a dry sense of humor, and I could make her laugh. Surely that was important in a relationship?

Relationship. That was the crucial word. Sharon had said Lee played the field. I had to accept that I was just another contestant.

There was a knock at the door. Before I opened it I knew it was Lee. She'd changed into jeans and a jade green shirt. She was restrained, serious. "Hi. Can I talk to you for a moment?"

I stood aside, gesturing towards the table. "There's still some coffee in the pot. If you don't mind using my cup . . ."

She smiled a little at that. "I kiss you. Why wouldn't I share your cup?"

Feeling awkward, ill at ease, but immeasurably pleased that she was here, I pulled up a second chair and poured the rest of the coffee for her. She sat, elbows on the table, cup held in both hands, scrutinizing my face.

"What?" I said.

"You should play poker — you've got the face for it."

I had a try at flippancy. "You're telling me I look blank?"

She sipped the coffee. "I'm saying I don't really know what you're thinking and feeling."

This was getting dangerous. I had a mad impulse, quickly stifled, to tell her the truth — that I was sliding, inexorably, incurably, in love with her. My words were more prosaic. "I'll order more coffee," I said. "Do you want anything else?"

While calling room service I watched her. She was uncharacteristically still, gazing out the window as I had been doing before. Even when sitting, she usually had an aura of vitality, but tonight that energy was dormant. When I came back to the table she said, "I'm sorry about this morning, Alex. I had no right to judge you."

I sighed. "I must seem a gutless wonder to you."

That made her smile. "A gutless wonder?" she repeated.

"I'm just not willing to let everyone know I'm a lesbian. I don't know what would happen if I did . . . Anyway, I'm not brave enough to give it a go."

A discreet knock at the door heralded the arrival of room service. I busied myself pouring a fresh cup each and putting crackers and cheese between us, as though these domestic actions would blunt the critical words I was sure she was about to voice.

But she was silent. At last I said, "Have you always been so open about yourself?"

"Not at first, but then — yes." She gave a tight smile. "Sorry, that was somewhat cryptic. I was sure I was a lesbian by the time I was sixteen, but I kept quiet. Maybe I thought it'd go away."

I wanted to know everything about her. "But . . ."

"When I was eighteen I fell in love — totally, disastrously in love — with Justine. And she with me." She looked down into her cup and was silent. I could imagine the memories parading past her eyes — and I was jealous of them.

"What happened?" I said reluctantly.

"Justine was terrified that someone might find out. She tried to run two lives. A secret one with me and another for the outside world. She had a boyfriend . . . just for show, she said, but she slept with him, and she slept with me. I told her I wouldn't share her, that she had to choose." She made a face. "She didn't choose me."

There was nothing to say that wouldn't sound trite, so I waited. Lee said, "I loved her so much ..." She shook her head. "Enough of the sticky emotion. After that, I came out. It seemed the right thing to do at the time — and it was. I've never regretted it." She reached over and touched my hand. "Alex, I'm not telling you that's what you should do, but it's been right for me. I'm free. No one can threaten me with disclosure, no one can try a little gentle blackmail. More than that, I've made a statement to myself about who I am." She released my hand and leaned back with a self-deprecating smile. "Sorry. Got on the soapbox for a moment, there."

"How did your parents take it?"

"Not very well. They were horrified and blamed themselves, of course. Where had they gone wrong? What had turned me into one of those women? But they love me, and eventually they accepted it. I'm not saying it was easy, Alex, but now I can be completely open with them — and that's worth the pain."

I looked away from her. "My parents would never forgive me, if they knew."

"You're close to them?"

"Close? No."

I'm not close to anyone, Lee. Can't you see that?

She pushed the chair back, stood up. "I'll go." She smiled mischievously. "We've both got to get at least *one* good night's sleep on this tour."

I kissed her at the door, as gently as I knew how. Held her lightly, carefully, as though she might break. But, of course, *I* was the one who was fragile, the one who would be broken by our affair.

CHAPTER TEN

I know the physical facts about Ayers Rock —
it's made of a red coarse-grained sandstone called
arkose that five hundred million years ago was part
of the sediment that formed the bed of an immense
inland sea. The huge shape rearing a thousand feet
above the plain is only the summit of a buried
mountain that goes perhaps ten thousand feet down
into a sea of sand. But the geology cannot explain
the impact that the Rock itself has.

I watched Lee's face as she saw Uluru — its
Aboriginal name — for the first time. Our flight

approached over sandy desert and suddenly there it was, a gigantic red monolith, its walls rising steeply, drenched in Dreamtime myth, brooding as it has for a million years over the flat featureless plain.

I wanted her to respond to its grandeur, but she was silent. At last I said, "What do you think?"

She shook her head. "Words don't describe it."

She was right, of course. And she would again find it hard to find words for the changes in color that the Rock displayed throughout the day. The first time I visited Uluru I watched the massive stone walls alter in the course of the day — brilliant red at sunrise, progressing through orange, crimson, purple, pastel shades, and lastly chocolate brown, before the desert night swept across the plains.

As our plane glided in to land, she said, "It's possible to climb to the top?"

"Yes, but it can be tough going."

"Will you come with me?"

I can't think of anywhere I wouldn't go with you.

"All right," I said.

The Uluru National Park is owned by the Aborigines, but administered in a lease-back agreement by the government. Our accommodation was twenty kilometers from Ayers Rock at the resort village of Yulara, "the place of the howling dingo." I always find the contrast bizarre. In harsh and ancient country dominated by the largest monolith in the world sits the technological luxury of air conditioning, television and swimming pools, complete with space-age parasol sails to shade pampered humans and direct the desert breezes to the best advantage. True, the resort is designed to blend in with the landscape, but essentially it trespasses upon an environment where, outside its comforts, every living thing, plant and animal, has a daily struggle just to survive.

Lee was unfazed by the information of how many people had managed to fall off the Rock — only a few — or who'd succumbed to heart attacks — rather more. She beamed at Tony. "You've never climbed it? It'll be a great experience."

"So you say," he said suspiciously. "I'd like a better idea of what's involved before I commit myself."

They both looked at me. "You want statistics? I have statistics." I ticked them off on my fingers: "It's six miles around the base. It covers nearly a thousand acres —"

Lee interrupted. "We're going up, not around."

"Unfair comment. I didn't want to waste any of the information I've memorized, but if you insist ... Ayers Rock is about twelve hundred feet high. The only safe route is marked. The actual distance covered is a mile and a half and two hours should be allowed to complete the round trip. Wear sensible clothing and non-slippery shoes. There's a general warning that it'll be a challenging task for anyone who's unfit."

"That's decided me," said Tony. "I don't want to die. You two are on your own. Mr. Wen has already set out with camera and tripod to photograph everything in sight."

I'd never climbed to the top of Uluru either, so the thrill of the challenge lifted my heart as we stood at the northwest corner of the base gazing up at the formidable sloping flanks looming above us.

The first ten minutes or so weren't too difficult,

but then the challenge of the climb became apparent. As we paused I said, "Trish and Suzie, friends of mine, climbed Uluru last year. They told me this point where we are now is called Chicken Rock, because if you're going to chicken out, you do it right now."

"I'm not going to chicken out. How about you, Alex?"

"Never."

I spoke boldly, but I felt decidedly nervous. It was all very well to know eighty-year-olds had bounded up the Rock like mountain goats, the truth was that the incline was now so steep that it would have been almost impossible without the knee-height chain that snaked its way up the red sandstone. Stern signs warned of fatal results if the chain were left to retrieve anything dropped. Half-crouching, buffeted by a malicious wind that suddenly swirled about us, we inched our way upwards. Rather, *I* inched — Lee, seemingly immune to the fear of falling that made me grip the chain compulsively, was way ahead of me.

I'd been told that this was the most difficult part of the climb, and I could believe it when I looked back over my shoulder, quailing at the thought of the descent.

The rest of the way was much less steep and I regained my initial enthusiasm. Lee forged ahead, moving with athletic grace. I caught up with her at a huge saddle of red rock before the final ascent, and together we reached the very top.

"Not bad, eh?" I said.

Lee spread her arms wide. "The space!"

The immense pale dome of the sky arched over

the bleak beauty of a primordial landscape baked by relentless light. We could see for hundreds of kilometers. To the west were the strange squat shapes of the Olgas and a range of hills called the Sedimentaries. The huge expanse of plain was dotted with clumps of spinifex grass, dark green mulga and mallee scrub — stubborn drought-resistant vegetation that provided shelter to an amazing variety of reptiles and birds, as well as rock wallabies, kangaroos and dingoes.

There was a cairn with a book where climbers recorded their achievement. I put my signature after Lee's, ridiculously pleased that there was now some permanent record of our names together.

Lee, restless, wanted to explore. "There are legends to do with the Rock?"

"You'll learn a whole lot more about the Aboriginal Dreamtime this afternoon when we take the guided tour of the paintings and rock carvings, but I know there's a waterhole that's the home of a huge mythical snake called Wanambi, the Rainbow Serpent. When it's provoked it rises out of the water and transforms itself into a rainbow that can kill whoever's offended it."

"I doubt you'd see a rainbow around here."

"Wrong. I did the first time I visited Uluru. Admittedly it doesn't happen often, but when it does it's spectacular. I remember the water poured off the Rock in torrents and within a few days desert flowers had sprung up everywhere. They only last a short time, and then they die, but their seeds lie in the earth waiting for the next rain."

She smiled at me, a smile so full of affection that

my heart faltered. "Alex, I wish I had more time to see your country with you."

"Could you stay longer?"

"No."

I had to make a joke of it — not let her see how much it mattered to me. "I forgot for a moment the Lee Paynter schedule comes first, second and last. Yes?"

"Something like that."

We found a spot out of the stiff breeze but where we could gaze out at the desert. We sat in companionable silence for a while, then Lee said, "You were married ..."

"Before I knew better."

"Would you tell me about it?"

Strangely, it was easy to talk about my parents and about Carl. She didn't ask questions, just glanced at me now and then. Most of the time she rested her chin on her knees and looked out towards the horizon. I told her more than I'd told anyone before, more than I'd ever intended to reveal.

Intimacy breeds intimacy: there is an unspoken rule that allowed me to ask Lee about her personal life. "After Justine ... has there been anyone important?"

She turned to face me. "I love women, Alex. I love their company and I love their bodies ... And sure, once or twice I thought there was something that would last, but it's never worked out. I don't think it's in me to have one, special person. My life is full and satisfying as it is."

This is a warning, isn't it, Lee? A warning not to get too involved, not to expect too much.

131

I said cheerfully, "Lots of appetizers and no main course, eh?"

She threw back her head and laughed. "I love it!" she said.

The climb to the top of Ayers Rock marked a change in our relationship. It was now a friendship — perhaps more than a friendship, because our intimacy in bed was being translated to a matching intimacy in our conversations.

During the afternoon we joined Tony and Mr. Wen and a group of other tourists as an Aboriginal ranger took us around the base of the Rock, explaining the significance of the rock carvings and the mythological beings depicted in them. I felt an intruder in an immense tapestry of folklore and legend that I couldn't fully comprehend. Juxtaposing two facts explained my sense of dislocation: Uluru had been central to the spiritual beliefs of Aboriginal tribes for forty thousand years; a white explorer, his heritage twelve thousand miles away in Europe, discovered and named it Ayers Rock after his uncle in the eighteen-seventies.

I tried to explain what I felt to Lee, half-expecting that she wouldn't understand. Short-changing people is a habit of mine — I've always avoided expecting too much, because that way I can't be disappointed. But Lee did understand. More, she could relate it to the effect the European exploration and settlement of her own country had had upon the Native Americans.

She was suddenly dear to me on a level I'd not

considered. Dimensions of her personality, of her mind, of her experiences stretched before me, all to be explored.

Dinner in the quietly luxurious dining room of the Sheraton Hotel featured emu and crocodile on the menu, to the delight of Mr. Wen. We were all relaxed with a pleasant fatigue and by the time coffee was served I found myself stifling a yawn. Mr. Wen, delighted with his photographic achievements during the day, insisted on describing the shots he'd taken and passing around the photographs he had developed of the Barrier Reef.

I looked around the table. We were like old friends lingering over a meal. I resented the fact that tomorrow Sir Frederick and the others would be arriving to disturb the links we had forged between us.

When we broke up to go to bed, I said to Lee in an appropriately light tone, "Your place or mine?"

She looked surprised. "There's a choice?"

I knew very well what she meant, but I still said, "Why wouldn't there be?"

She looked at me gravely. "Because, Alex, if you come to me, you can leave when you want to, and that gives you control."

"Come to my room."

She grinned. "Okay, but don't try and throw me out in the middle of the night. I won't budge."

A beautiful languorous sensuality possessed me. I sat astride Lee, leaning over her, my lips brushing her face, my fingers buried in her hair, gently caressing. I raised my head. Her eyes were shut, her lips curved with pleasure. I could feel the bones of her skull, the vertebrae in her neck, the flat planes of her shoulders.

She stretched, purred under my touch, pulled me down to her. We kissed, deeply, slowly — exploring, probing. I held her face in my hands, traced its lines with my tongue, words that couldn't be spoken swelling in my throat.

It was an aching sweetness to feel the heavy throb of her pulse against my fingers. Desire burned in me, but it was a patient, leisurely warmth. The palms of my hands brushed against her breasts, teasing her nipples until they were taut.

Head back, eyes closed, Lee began to quiver as her hips lifted under me. "Alex," she breathed. My own name was a fire along my thighs. I wanted to murmur impossible endearments. Tell her how the very essence of me loved her ...

I moved down her body, my hands, mouth, skin learning her secrets. For a moment, I broke contact.

"Don't leave me — don't stop."

Sliding off the end of the bed, I knelt, pulled her towards me. She drew her knees up, opened fully to me. It was delicious, the smell, the taste, the response that her body gave me. My tongue tantalized, touching gently, tentatively, then, as my fingers within her were clenched in a tighter and tighter embrace, I grew fiercer, more demanding.

I could hear inarticulate sounds as she arched, vibrated. My arm was under her, clasping her against the wet heat of my mouth. Then she drew in her breath and was poised, silent, waiting.

"Alex!" The tremors that shook her were violent, consuming — and I was consumed by my name.

"I love you," I said, knowing she couldn't hear me through the storm of orgasm.

I couldn't believe I'd ever say it again.

CHAPTER ELEVEN

The flight from the Top End bringing Sir Frederick, Steve, Hilary Ferguson and several others from the convention were due early in the morning. I hoped we could leave for the Olgas before they arrived at the hotel, but it was a vain wish. As we waited for our transportation with a group of other tourists and our guide, Sir Frederick came striding into the lobby. Heads turned — he was a suave, distinguished figure and his clipped English accent cut through the murmur of conversation. "Glad I caught you before you went out. What's your program for today?"

As the others from his party straggled in he said to them, "They're off to the Olgas, and since we've only got one day at Uluru, I fancy some of you might want to go with them."

The company of strangers was one thing — the presence of Steve, Hilary et al. was another. "It's best to climb Ayers Rock in the morning," I suggested helpfully.

Hilary looked startled at the very concept of scaling the monolith. Steve brushed aside the suggestion. "I've climbed it, and it's bloody hard yakka. And hardly worth the trouble when you get to the top. We'll come with you to the Olgas."

I sighed to myself. I had wanted to spend one more unfettered day with Lee, but this idea was rapidly evaporating. Perversely, I said, "Are you coming too, Sir Frederick?"

His pleasure at my suggestion made it obvious I'd made a serious error of judgment — the last thing I should be doing was encouraging him. "Alexandra, such a pity. I've several urgent calls to make. But we'll all get together later."

The drive to the Olgas took less than an hour. I was last onto the bus and so took the only vacant seat next to a stranger. Our guide, a cheerful Aboriginal man who looked as spare and resilient as the desert vegetation he was describing, pointed out the huge clumps of needle-sharp spinifex grass, the striking orange-flowered grevillea shrubs, bloodwoods, mulga and desert oak.

My spirits lifted when we approached the eight

square miles of fantasy that were the Olgas. To me the rounded shapes of the thirty-five or so huge rock domes scattered in a semi-circle around a central valley are beguilingly feminine, although the Aboriginal name Katatjuta has the prosaic meaning of "many heads." As old as Ayers Rock, they're made of an entirely different material — a conglomerate that includes boulders, sand and pebbles, all bound together like a cake mix. Like the Rock, they change in color during the day, turning to deepest purple in the late afternoon. Now, in mid-morning, they were a soft violet-pink.

"They remind me of gigantic stone puddings," I said to Tony as we began our trek from the car park through the Olga Gorge towards the Valley of the Winds.

It was a beautiful morning to be walking under the gaze of the towering globes. The metallic heat of the sun was tempered by a gentle breeze, a wedge-tailed eagle spiraled overhead on a thermal updraft, and on a slope above us two red kangaroos rested on their muscular tails and regarded our party with wide, soft eyes.

As someone exclaimed over a ferocious-looking thorny devil sunbaking on a rock, Tony took my arm. "I need to talk to you."

We waited until the others had passed us and we could bring up the rear. I took off my sunglasses. "A problem with work?"

"No, not exactly. It's what I was discussing with Lee on the flight to Alice Springs."

Thinking of the way he'd dismissed me at the airport when I'd raised the subject, I said tartly, "So what's decided you to let me in on the secret?"

"Lee has."

I waited. It was hot, and Tony stopped to mop his flushed face. Then he said, "This is confidential."

"Of course."

"Well, although it's going to sound impossibly dramatic, the fact is ... Steve's trying to blackmail me. I don't mean for money — it's more subtle than that. It's for preference in promotion. He's after the Asian job and he knows Sir Frederick will consult with me about it. He's demanding that I recommend he gets it."

My astonishment didn't show in my voice. I said coolly, "What's he got on you?"

He let his breath out in a long sigh. "I'm gay."

"But you've been married ..." It was a stupid thing to say. *I'd* been married, too.

Tony obviously shared my view. Anger washed across his face. "Of all people, Alex, *you* should know how little that could mean."

Seeing my expression change, he added quickly, "No one told me — I already knew."

"*How?*"

"Relax, the others don't know. It was little things, they all added up. And I saw you once, in a gay bar ..." He gave a short, bitter laugh. "I hid from you, would you believe."

Prickling with unease, I said, "Steve ... how did he find out about you?"

"Sheer bad luck — Steve went to school with a guy who knew my ... friend. There was a reunion, they got to talking ..."

"Why are you telling me this now?"

"I get on well with Lee and I told her I was gay on one of the A.P.P. business trips to the States.

139

Steve's only put the screws on in the last few weeks, so I discussed the whole situation with her on the flight from Cairns to Alice Springs."

I was tight with anxiety. "You haven't answered my question."

"If Steve finds out you're a lesbian, he'll use it — not just because he's a nasty bit of work, but because the promotion to the new position's basically between the two of you. And it's pretty obvious you're a front runner with Sir Frederick."

"Steve's been positively encouraging about Sir Frederick ... Tells me a proposal of marriage is in the offing."

Tony's tight smile matched my cynical tone. "If you ask me, he wants you to step out of line, make a play for the boss, and get dumped for your trouble."

"It's more likely he thinks Sir Frederick wouldn't promote me if we had a personal involvement. It would look bad."

Tony shrugged. "Whatever the reasoning Steve uses, he's still dangerous."

"Was it Lee's idea that you should warn me?"

"Not exactly. I asked her opinion about telling you."

I stared at him, wondering if he knew that we were lovers. He seemed to read my mind. "You and Lee? I guessed that too. She hasn't said a word to me, but the way you look at her ..."

"God. Is it that obvious?"

He touched the side of my face, a gentle, affectionate gesture. "No, Alex. Only to friends who love you."

* * * * *

I anticipated that dinner that night would be trying, but, as often happens, an expected ordeal turned out to be a very pleasant occasion. I was careful to sit away from Lee — Tony's acuity about my relationship with her had alarmed and depressed me. If he could guess the truth, why couldn't somebody else? And if that somebody happened to be Steve ...

Sir Frederick insisted on champagne to mark our last night in the Outback before we returned to Sydney. Also, he had a fund of droll stories culled from his travel experiences around the world, and he recounted these with his usual oratorical skill. We laughed our way through our meal, everyone contributing to the effervescent atmosphere. After coffee Sir Frederick announced that Tony, who was, he said expansively, an astronomical expert, would be taking us outside for star-gazing.

Away from the lights of the resort, the sky seemed weighted down with stars. They burned with a cold, crystalline glitter — whirling galaxies unimaginable distances away. Lee was close to me, and in the darkness I took her hand. Our fingers interlocked, and a sharp joy filled me.

Tony was explaining how to locate the constellation of the Southern Cross by finding the bright pointer stars. I stared up at the pattern of five scintillating dots of light that can always be used to find true south, no matter where they are in the sky. "Don't wish — you might get what you ask for," is one of my mother's more cynical admonitions.

My fingers tightened around Lee's, and, ignoring my mother's advice, I wished with all my heart, as if, for once, reality could be defeated.

When we went inside, I remained carefully apart from Lee. I found myself looking for Steve, assessing his expression, wondering what he was thinking. I'd never trusted his slick friendliness, but now my mild aversion had ripened into contempt. Of course none of this showed. I talked and joked with him just as normal, although part of me despised my accommodation.

Sir Frederick, mellowed by champagne, told me to call him "Frederick." I smiled, but it was a request I had no intention of obeying. It was tiresome — now I'd have to indulge in verbal gymnastics to avoid using his name at all.

Quite late, people began to drift off to bed. A casual glance from Lee, a slight nod from me, and we communicated. Although it warmed me that this could happen — that our understanding was such that only a subtle exchange was needed — my pleasure was diminished by apprehension. However much I argued with myself, it made a difference to me that Sir Frederick and Steve were at the hotel.

I couldn't forget the past. The memory of the last time I'd seen Zoe after she'd been forced to resign kept playing in my head. She had cried — the first time I ever saw her defeated. "The bastards, the bastards," she'd said. "You can't beat them, Alex. They'll always win in the end."

It angered me that I felt I had to check the corridor before I went to Lee's room. Although we hadn't discussed it, there was an unspoken agreement that I would go to her, not she to me. When she opened her door I slipped inside like an accomplice to some crime.

"Are you sure you should be here, Alex? Sir Frederick may be checking your room."

There was more sarcasm than playfulness in her tone, but I chose to ignore the sting in her remark.

I said, "Tony's told me about Steve."

"And?"

"When did you know I was a lesbian?"

Strangely, I'd never asked her this before. Lee seemed to realize the anxiety that drove me to the question. "I wouldn't have known ... there was nothing you did or said." Smiling, she added, "Of course, I had high hopes."

Irritated by her light tone, I said, "Are you telling me the truth?"

"In a manner of speaking. I felt a tug of attraction for you ... that's usually significant." She frowned at my expression. "Don't worry about it. You're a natural conspirator."

"Somehow I don't think that's a compliment." When she didn't respond I said rashly, "I know what you're thinking."

Eyebrows raised, she said with a tone of polite doubt, "You do?"

"You believe that if we both came out of the closet everything'd be fine. Well, it wouldn't be, Lee. If it was that easy, don't you think I'd have done it long ago?"

Shrugging, she said, "Perhaps you enjoy the intrigue."

I was growing angry and defensive. "I can't afford any suspicion — I mean, Steve will use anything he can get."

"You're going to let Steve Monahan dictate what you do and don't do?"

Smarting from her scorn, I snapped, "It's not like that."

"No? What *is* it like?"

A tide of anger and grief rose in my throat. "You'll be gone, soon. But I have to live here, work here ... It'll make a difference to my life, make it impossible. Can't you see that?"

"I can see you believe that."

"You must love the high moral ground — you spend so much time there."

She said sardonically, "A hit, a very palpable hit."

"And don't ..." I said savagely as I opened the door, "... quote bloody Shakespeare at me!"

CHAPTER TWELVE

It was raining in Sydney, an outrageous event that immediately put me into an even darker mood. One of the great experiences of travel is to fly into my harbor city on a fine, sunny day when all its beauty is displayed to the best advantage. Shrouded in curtains of heavy gray rain, Sydney was like any other large, wet metropolis.

I'd avoided Lee since our fruitless argument and, miserably aware that she had only a few days left in Australia, I spent the first night at home trying to persuade myself that my infatuation for her was just that — an intense, but short-lived affair.

My modest little house had been a refuge, but now it felt like a prison. I knew where she was staying, and I picked up the phone a hundred times, it seemed, to speak with her, but put the receiver down each time.

It was unrealistic to hope she might call me — and she didn't.

It was still raining the next day as I went to work in a haze of unhappiness. A.P.P.'s head office was in a restored sandstone building of minor, but distinct, historic importance, overlooking the Royal Botanic Gardens and just up the hill from the gigantic curving roofs of the Opera House, an appropriate position for a tourist organization.

I sat in Tony's office glaring morosely at the wet world outside. Tony patted my shoulder. "You'd better cheer up for the big do tonight."

He was referring to the formal banquet A.P.P. was hosting for state and federal tourist bodies and important private tour companies, plus any overseas wholesalers from the convention who were still in Sydney. It was to be held at the Regent near the Circular Quay — the hotel at which Lee was staying.

"I can't wait," I said quite inaccurately. I didn't want to go.

What was the point in dragging the whole thing out? She'd be gone in a few days and the truth was brutally clear: I cared too much — she didn't care enough. Or, to be more honest, Lee had remained true to her philosophy while I had broken every rule I'd made for myself to live by.

I'd come into Tony's office as a respite from my own small cubicle, where work I didn't want to do was piling up and where Steve could — and did — pop in for a chat at regular intervals. I hid the intense anger I felt about his attempts to blackmail Tony as we engaged in the usual office banter. And I was vigilant for the double meaning, the needling comment that would show he knew about Lee. There was nothing — his manner was the same as always, friendly, irreverent and egocentric.

The burr of Tony's phone broke into my thoughts. He picked it up and swiveled his chair to look out the rain-spotted window. My attention swung to him as he said, "Lee. Hi! Yes, she's here. I'll put her on." Handing me the receiver he said with a grin, "I'll leave you two alone."

It was amazing what one name could do. Suddenly the day looked brighter, I could swear it was fining up.

"Alex? You're going to the banquet tonight, aren't you?"

"Yes."

"I wondered if we could make a date for afterwards."

Why not? You can't get in any deeper.

"Would that be in your room?"

"Why, yes," said Lee, laughing. "How astute of you." Then, more seriously, "Alex, I wanted to call you last night, but . . ."

"But?"

I heard her sigh. "Just but . . ."

I felt agitated, tormented. If she was worried about encouraging me, why was she suggesting we meet? If only she cared enough . . .

147

To love you? Dream on, Alex.
I said lightly, "It's a date."

I prepared for the banquet with special care, selecting a deep rose dress that had been one of those serendipitous finds — it seemed to have been made just for me, enhancing whatever qualities are mine so that when I have it on I feel relaxed and attractive. I don't usually wear jewelry, but tonight I put on a thin gold necklace and gold earrings.

Tony was accompanying me. I thought how great he looked when he arrived. Even the most insignificant men — and Tony is hardly that — gain consequence when dressed formally. His ample body was transformed into an impressive, powerful presence just by the addition of a starched shirt, black tie and a well-cut formal suit.

"Magnificent is the word that springs to mind," I said as I opened the door to him.

"You're not so bad yourself. In fact, I might go so far as to say you look pretty terrific." His smile faded. "A fine couple of hypocrites we are, Alex. We'll walk in looking the perfect couple . . ."

It was unfair of him to spoil my anticipation of the evening. "Ah, come on! Forget it — let's just eat, drink and be merry." I couldn't help adding: "For tomorrow we may come out of the closet."

In the car, Tony was somber. "Alex, you need to know something. Lee says that if she were me, she'd go to Sir Frederick right now. She thinks that sooner or later Steve will come out with it anyway, and I agree. He's a vicious little prick and he won't be able to stop himself."

I didn't want to discuss this, but I could hardly sit mute. "Are you going to?"

"Yes. As soon as things quiet down and we unload the last overseas visitor." When I didn't say anything, he went on, "Don't worry — you won't be involved. There's no reason you should be. In fact, the whole thing'll be to your advantage, because if Sir Frederick believes me, at the very least Steve's blown his chance of promotion."

"*If* he believes you!"

"I don't think Sir Frederick's got much time for queers. Mind you, I might be unfair — it's hardly a subject I've ever discussed with him."

We sat in silence for the rest of the trip.

Pre-dinner drinks were well under way when we arrived. Sir Frederick, looking extremely distinguished, greeted us at the door, and immediately dispatched us to whisper sweet commercial nothings into selected politicians' ears. My mark was a weedy little man wearing a suit a size too large who was the exception to my rule that formal wear improves male appearance. He had recently gained the state tourism portfolio, a position to which he had been appointed by virtue of his propensity to back the right politician in the leadership stakes. "Charming," he said, eying my cleavage.

Eventually I was rescued by a syndicated journalist who reported on travel for several major newspapers. As this particular politician was a ruthless self-promoter who gave the impression he would rather talk to the press than to his own nearest and dearest, my escape was easy.

I searched the crowd for Lee, finding her on the other side of the room in a knot of laughing people. She wore black, which was sensational with her blonde hair. She stepped away from the others to greet me. Looking me up and down, she said softly, "Wow."

"I bet you say that to all the girls."

"Only you."

"Lee! Alex! The two most stunning sheilas in the room!"

Steve looked pretty stunning himself. To be truthful, he looked magnificent. His height and tanned skin, not to mention his fair hair, were more than enhanced by formal wear. "Why waste your time talking to each other? The place is loaded with eligible men."

"You being one of them?"

He put his arm around my waist. "You know I am, Alex, darling. Don't fight it."

I removed his encircling arm.

He turned to Lee with his warmest smile. "I just happen to have come across a special South Australian outback safari you might be interested in . . ."

My astonishment must have shown on my face, but he was careful not to look at me, knowing full well he was breaking A.P.P. protocol by making a direct approach when Lee Paynter was my responsibility.

She said briskly, "Yes? What are the details?"

He gestured expansively. "The tour covers the

Birdsville Track and the wetlands of the Coongie Lakes, not to mention the Andamooka opal fields . . ."

"The tour operator? Credentials?"

"Just a small outfit — but I've heard it's reliable."

"You've heard?" repeated Lee. Her curt tone seemed to disconcert Steve, and I began to feel a certain wry amusement. Working with him had made me aware how often he was tempted to wing it — to scrimp on his homework and rely on bluff and charm to get him through.

"Well, the broad picture is —"

"I want specifics."

Steve reddened. "Of course . . ."

She ignored his discomfort, asking a series of sharp questions about cost factors, tour frequency, connection flights, standards of transport, accommodation, inclusions and extras.

When it became obvious that he was floundering, she said contemptuously, "Why don't you come back, sonny, when you've got hard information and some numbers for me to crunch?"

I almost felt embarrassed for him until I remembered how entertaining he had always found other people's humiliation.

Steve swallowed, passed a hand over his hair, said with an attempt at nonchalance, "Right. I'll get back to you, then."

"You do that."

A discreet bell rang to indicate that we should start moving into the banquet room. Giving a muttered excuse, he stepped aside. Concealing my delight, I glanced at Lee. She looked imperturbable, as though her castigation of Steve had never occurred.

The meal was what one might truly call "a sumptuous repast." I was seated with a group of established travel professionals and we regaled each other with in-jokes and stories about the industry — or rather, *they* regaled and I listened with fluctuating attention. Lee had three more days in Sydney and I oscillated between an ardent desire to be near her and a distinct fear of the potential hurt that closeness might bring.

The banquet, as Sir Frederick was bound to assure me the next day, met every expectation. For me, much of the evening passed in a blur of speeches, toasts and waiters neatly placing, or alternatively whisking away, plates and glasses.

Sir Frederick expected us to stay until the last stragglers left, and I was burning with impatience when the opportunity to slip away at last arrived.

There was only a moment between my knock and Lee opening the door, and I was in her arms almost before she'd shut it behind me. "What took you so long?"

I shut my eyes, breathing in the scent of her. "Oh, I don't know ... I had better things to do than rush up here to you."

She chuckled — that warm, deep laugh that I treasured. "Well, Alex, do you want anything? A drink? A shower, perhaps? A look at the view?"

"I want you. Just you."

She'd changed into a silky blue robe and when I undid the belt and slid my hands under it I touched her warm, bare skin. "Darling," I said, aware that it was the first endearment I'd ever used with her.

Why was it that in the past, other women had only stirred my body, but when Lee touched me it was more, much more? I loved her physically, yes, but the essential Lee, the *person* — I admired, respected, cherished, adored.

Can I love you this much, Lee, and not have you love me too . . . just a little?

Lee was engaged in undressing me while driving me frantic with her hands and mouth. Her tongue was tracing delicate patterns . . . the hollow of my throat, the line of my collarbone . . . then, undoing my bra, she began sucking, gently biting, my breasts.

Cupping her buttocks, I pulled her hard against me. "Bed," I said. "I'm not up to the floor."

I shuddered from the feel of the whole length of her against my body — and then she was turning me, holding me with surprising strength. "Let me have my wicked way with you, Alex!"

"Anything. I'm yours."

Her hands became gentle, slow. She caressed my hips, stroked my thighs — patterns of sensation that grew in intensity as they were repeated.

At last her fingers drew nearer, circled, yet didn't reach my clitoris. I was swollen, bursting, curved like a bow before an arrow is loosed. "Please!' My teeth clenched, the blood thudding in my ears, I was centered on that one urgency.

My body leaped at her first deep touch. "Yes!"

She was kneeling beside me, her mouth on mine, her fingers deep within me, her thumb stroking a tight rhythm. And my hips were moving in accord, thrusting against the pulse of her hand.

Light flared behind my eyes as I surged to the momentary balance between joy and desire. My labored breathing became a series of gasps, and then, from deep within me, the tremors began, their urgent tempo wrenching a cry from my tight throat.

It wasn't stopping. "Oh, God, Lee . . ."

My body bucked to continuous, exquisite, unbearable spasms.

Then I was soaked in sweat, struggling for breath, smiling in her arms. "I liked that," I said.

Much later I woke alone in the bed. I squinted at the illuminated dial of the bedside clock: three-thirty.

Lee was standing by the window, the diffuse light from outside casting an aura around her. I untangled myself from the sheets and went to stand behind her, sliding my arms around her waist. My breasts pressing against the cool skin of her back, my chin resting on her shoulder, I gazed with her at the floodlit sails of the Opera House and the silent Circular Quay wharfs, stilled from the busy clamor of the day.

At last I said, "What's up?"

"Alex, I'm flying home later today. I had a call before the banquet. There's a major problem with an important deal, and I need to be there."

Don't make a fool of yourself, Alex . . . it's over.

My throat was so constricted my voice sounded

alien and strained. "There's something I have to say."

She moved in protest. "No, don't."

"I can't *not* say it, now that you're going."

I felt her tense in my arms. Miserable, driven, I said, "I love you. You must know I love you."

She turned to face me. "Alex, I care, but not that way."

Stop now. Don't say anything else.

"Lee, I love you so much. I can't believe you don't return at least some of it."

She sounded firm, detached. "I can't love you the way you want to be loved. I can't."

There was a long, long silence. At last Lee said, "At least, can't we —"

"Be friends? You're not going to ask that?"

In the dim light I saw her hesitant, unhappy smile. "Well, yes, I was ..."

"That's not an option."

I turned away, began to collect my clothes. "What time's your flight? I'll drive you out to the airport."

"Alex, that's not necessary."

I stopped and looked at her. "It is. It's rather like a funeral. You need to go through the formal goodbyes."

I'd gone home, hadn't even tried to snatch any sleep, had showered and dressed. I would be going back to the office after I'd taken Lee to the airport, so I put on a conservative dark dress, thinking sardonically that perhaps I should wear black.

I knew that eventually the feeling of sharp loss would penetrate my fatigue, but for the moment I was grateful for my tiredness. Lee's flight left shortly after noon, so by mid-morning I was back at the Regent Hotel.

She was waiting beside her luggage as I drew up, and I thought bitterly that it was obvious she'd wanted to avoid meeting me in the intimacy of her room. We looked at each other silently. What was there left to say?

I found it ironic that the route to the airport took us along Southern Cross Drive. Out in the desert I'd wished upon the Southern Cross, but my wish had decidedly not come true.

Lee was twisting her fingers together. I'd never seen her show any sign of nervousness or tension before — perhaps she was feeling as wretched as I.

She said abruptly, "Alex, it could never have worked out. I mean, you have your career here in Australia, and I'm based in the States."

"My career's in international tourism. Something would have been possible.

"You'd leave Australia?"

"It'll always be here to come back to ... and for you, Lee, I'd go anywhere."

She bent her head. "I'm sorry."

I was filled with a corrosive anger. "In the past haven't other women fallen in love with you? Do you have a lot of practice in telling them to get lost?"

Tight-lipped, she said, "I make the ground rules clear, and I get out if it looks like anyone's getting too serious."

"Is that why you're leaving today? You've

manufactured a crisis so you can extricate yourself from a sticky situation?"

Obviously stung, she turned to me, saying emphatically, "I haven't manufactured anything. I *wanted* to stay longer and I was sorry when I found I couldn't. I like being with you very much."

"Not enough, it appears."

"Alex, if I could give you the love you need, I would."

I felt like a kid denied a longed-for present. Childishly, I asked, "Why can't you?"

She was upset. A tremor ran through her voice. "Alex, if I were to love anyone like that, it would be you. But it's impossible. I can't, and I won't, make a commitment to you or to anyone else."

My head had begun to ache with slow, painful throbs. "This is futile," I said.

She'd regained control of herself. "Yes, it is. I can't change the way I am."

The crowded airport was a kaleidoscope of fragmented pictures: weeping people parting; raucous groups farewelling envied peers; sober business travelers; technicolor vacationers set for holiday destinations. And people were happy, unhappy, bored, excited, impatient, confused.

My job meant that I was more familiar with airports, particularly Sydney's busy terminal. Up to now I'd been indifferent to its noise and crowds and the extraordinary amount of luggage that people are willing to cart around with them. Today I hated everything about it.

Lee checked in her suitcases, paid the departure tax and, having run out of things to occupy her, stood with me in front of the passenger entrance to customs. "Alex, I don't want to lose contact with you."

"I imagine we'll communicate at times through A.P.P."

"That's not what I meant ..."

I said forcefully, "That's all you'll get." Then, more modestly, "I'm not trying to be difficult, I just can't bear it."

She looked at me with those gray, steady eyes that I loved. I touched her cheek with my fingertips, then leaned forward and kissed her lightly on the mouth. We said nothing else. She turned and walked away from me.

CHAPTER THIRTEEN

I'd come into Tony's office to give him some papers. He asked me to shut the door, then said flatly, "I'm going to tell him today."

We'd had a month of frenzied work at A.P.P. after the convention — tying up loose ends for overseas clients, negotiating over the invariable hitches that occurred with some deals, liaising between Australian companies and their overseas counterparts. For much of the time Steve had been in Japan working on a proposal to have influential businessmen join well-known Australian golfers on a tour of our most prestigious courses. Before Steve had left Australia Tony had told him that he had no intention of supporting his promotion.

It was Friday. Steve was due back on Monday. Tony said derisively, "I'd better give Sir Frederick the weekend to absorb the shock, so if Steve decides to dob me in it'll be old news."

Trying to reassure myself as well as Tony, I said, "Maybe you don't need to go ahead with this. After all, we don't know for sure that Steve's going to say anything."

He shrugged. "I'm telling Sir Frederick anyway, because if it isn't Steve, it'll be someone else."

Anxiety and anger combined to make my voice louder than I intended. "I'll stand behind you on this. You don't have to face it alone. If you need me, I'll be there."

He leaned over to touch my hand. "Alex, thank you, but you don't have to be dragged into this."

I thought of Zoe, whom I'd let face the music alone. "I am involved. It's my issue too, remember."

"There's no reason for you to be mentioned."

I wanted so much to say that I'd go in with him, tell Sir Frederick I was a lesbian, come out of the closet and to hell with the consequences ... but I couldn't.

He rubbed his eyes with the heels of his hands. Sounding resigned, he said, "This could be hello world — and goodbye job."

My resentment and anger at the unfairness of it all went up a notch. "You've got the law on your side, Tony, both State and Commonwealth. You know you can't be discriminated against on the grounds of sexual preference."

He grinned sourly. "True. I can't imagine Sir Frederick would like to see me waltzing into the Human Rights and Equal Opportunity Commission — the publicity would be murder." His smile faded. "If there's going to be a problem, it'll be more subtle than that."

A sharp rap at the door and Jackie Luff bustled officiously into the office. "Tony, these are all urgent queries from Japan." She turned her attention to me. "And here's another fax from Lee Paynter for you."

Lee's name always made my heart jump, but I knew that any communication would be business. Over the last weeks I'd chased up information for her company, and we'd sent faxes to each other regularly, all of them scrupulously professional.

I wished I could ask Sir Frederick to assign Lee's company to someone else, but I could think of no possible excuse that would persuade him, particularly as he was convinced that my working relationship with her was an excellent one.

I went back to my desk, looked at the pile of papers obscuring my in-tray, glanced at the fax Jackie had given me ... and thought of Lee. She filled my dreams, she impinged on my life in so many ways. Even when I pushed her out of my mind, all I needed was to hear an American accent like hers, or see a woman with tawny blonde hair, or notice a certain way of walking, or a turn of head — and she was back on center stage.

Without her, my life had no flavor. I could remind myself that before I met her I'd been content, but it had become obvious to me that I could never go back completely to that sterile existence.

I grieved, more than I'd have thought possible, and in my despair I turned to my friends, suddenly aware of how few in number they were. I had dinner with Tony and his partner, Paul, and delighted in the different perspective I had of his life. I went to the movies with Sharon, and was tempted to tell her about myself and Lee — but didn't. Most of all, I saw my dear friends Trish and Suzie, finding that I could talk to them about Lee, but not in any detail.

"Why weren't we introduced to this woman?" said Suzie with some indignation.

"There wasn't time — and besides, you're too good-looking."

Suzie had the endearing quality of always believing compliments, so she nodded, convinced by my excuse.

Constantly, no matter where I was or what I was doing, I wanted Lee. Sometimes I imagined that she must know how I felt and that the power of my emotions could transcend time and space. Mostly, I just endured my unhappiness.

And of course there was work to fill up my time. I'd had to make several interstate trips, there were serious difficulties with a large West Australian tour company, and we'd had a new computer system installed in the office. Dealing with all these problems meant that when I got home to my lonely little house I was too tired to do anything much but eat, watch television in a desultory way, shower and go to bed.

Whatever else she'd done, Lee had changed me. I wished I could tell her what an excellent role model she'd been. Her self-acceptance, her openness about her sexual identity, the sheer freedom from fear of discovery that she had — all these made me see how narrow and closeted my life was. And with that insight, there grew in me a desire to be as free as she.

Tony had made an appointment to see Sir Frederick late on this Friday afternoon. I clasped his hand before he went in. "Give a yell if you need me."

Tense, unable to concentrate on anything else, I kept watching the office door, listening for raised voices. When, after half an hour, Tony came out, his expression was bleak.

I took a deep breath. "What happened?"

"What can I say? Sir Frederick wasn't ecstatic . . . but then again, he didn't recoil with horror, either. Frankly, he seemed vaguely disappointed in me."

"And about Steve?"

Tony's lips tightened. "He heard me out, but he didn't believe me. Told me I must be mistaken, had taken a joking comment from Steve the wrong way . . ."

I was enraged. I didn't stop to think. "Come on, we're going back in there!"

My fury must have been obvious. Sir Frederick half rose from his chair. "Alexandra?"

"You don't believe what Tony told you about Steve!"

Sir Frederick sank back into his chair, irritation

flickering across his face. "I can't see this concerns you, Alexandra. It seems to me a misunderstanding between Tony and Steve."

"A misunderstanding?" I said furiously. "You think an attempt to blackmail Tony by threatening to tell everyone he's homosexual is a *misunderstanding?*"

Sir Frederick reddened with anger. "Leave it be. I've had all I can handle for the time being."

Tony said, "Alex . . ."

I ignored him. Armored by my fury, I locked eyes with Sir Frederick. "You don't mistake a threat like that if you're hiding the fact that you're gay. I know, firsthand."

His chin went up. "Firsthand?"

A giddy sense of freedom swept through me. "Yes, I've been through it. And I wasn't as brave as Tony. I didn't tell the truth about myself."

Sir Frederick looked away. "I see."

"I don't think you do. Can you imagine what it's like to live in a world where you have to pretend to be part of it? And when someone like Steve finds out your secret, what a weapon he has to use against you . . . as long as you let him get away with it."

Sir Frederick looked uncharacteristically weary. The famous ramrod posture was wilting a little, and even his bristling white mustache seemed to droop. "I see," he said again. Then, looking back at me, he gave a faint, ironic smile. "This explains a lot of things . . ."

My anger evaporated in astonishment. With wry amusement I realized that he was referring to my lack of enthusiasm for his well-mannered pursuit of me.

It was my turn to feel weary. Sliding my arm through Tony's, I took my leave of Sir Frederick.

It was late. Everyone had gone when we came out of Sir Frederick's office.

"Alex, you didn't need to do that ... but thank you."

I put an arm around Tony's waist. Hugged him. "How do you feel?"

"You won't believe it, but I feel great. No, more than great — exhilarated, because I'm free." He took my hands. "Everyone will know about me, but Sir Frederick will keep quiet about you if you ask him to. There's no need for you to make a statement on my behalf."

"Typical male conceit," I said. "Any statement I make is for me — not you."

CHAPTER FOURTEEN

In the weeks following Tony's admission, some things changed. For example, Sir Frederick now treated him with reserve, ostentatious in never touching him, whereas previously he'd often clapped him on the shoulder. And there were a few snide remarks — but none from Steve, who had apparently been spoken to by Sir Frederick. Some people were embarrassed or cool, but overall Tony seemed to have weathered the worst of it.

For myself, everything was very low-key. I felt no

compulsion for confrontation, but had decided to be open if anyone asked me directly. No one did, although every now and then I caught Steve looking at me speculatively, and there were a few awkward moments when I inadvertently intruded upon hushed conversations that were obviously about me or Tony.

And there was the problem of my parents.

"Are you going to tell them?" Tony asked.

"Sooner or later — preferably later."

His smile was sympathetic. "They'll cope. And if they don't — I guarantee they'll come round eventually."

I thought of my mother's cold rigidity, my father's self-righteousness, and a spurt of anger toughened my resolve. "Actually," I said caustically, "I was thinking of telling them when I go down to Canberra at Christmas time. It would be my present to them ..."

One afternoon after work I sat with Sharon in a cramped coffee shop watching people hurry home. She was meeting her husband for dinner and a show, and had an hour to kill. As I didn't have any reason to rush back to my empty house, I was happy to keep her company.

We chatted about this and that, and then Sharon brought up the subject of Tony being gay. She was so warmly supportive of him and contemptuous of some of our colleagues' reactions that I decided to speak out.

I said, "Sharon, I suppose you've heard I'm gay, too?"

She grinned at me. "That must have been quite a scene in Sir Frederick's office."

"It was." I toyed with my spoon. "I suppose there's been a certain amount of gossip ..."

"Sure there has, but it'll die down."

"Do you think coming out will affect Tony's career — and mine?"

She ran her hands through her mane of red hair. "Possibly — even probably. There'll always be someone who has a problem with anyone different, but if you ask me, I think you've done the right thing. When it's out in the open, no one can run a whispering campaign, or undermine you to the boss."

"You know about Steve?"

Her tone was scornful. "Slippery little bastard, isn't he? But he's made a major miscalculation this time. I gather Sir Frederick tore strips off him."

"He'll survive."

Sharon nodded agreement. "Of course he will. His type always does. But it's nice to see it blow up in his face, just this once."

The next day was bright and sunny. I strayed from my desk to stand at a window and gaze out over the Royal Botanic Gardens, as though the cool green of vegetation would soothe my dark thoughts. First thing that morning Sir Frederick had told me that neither Steve nor I would get the Asian position. It had gone to an outsider. I'd wanted something to be a goal in my life, something to hope for, and that job had been the focus of my attention.

Jackie Luff broke into my thoughts. "Sir Frederick wants to see you, Alex." When I didn't respond immediately, she added righteously, "Right now."

Since the scene in his office, there had been a hint of awkwardness in Sir Frederick's manner towards me. He gestured for me to sit down. "I've just had a call from Lee Paynter. She's flying to Sydney next week. As you know, her company's first Australian tour is at the end of the month. I don't understand why she finds it necessary to come out here. Is there a problem I don't know about?"

"No. Everything's going smoothly. Did she give a reason?"

"Said something about overseeing the tour, but that's not credible. She'd send an off-sider to do that. I'm concerned there *is* a problem, and she's not telling me what it is, so I'd like you to clear your appointments and be available for the whole time she's here."

I was shocked. "I'm supposed to fly to Perth —"

"Someone else can go. This is more important. I've asked Jackie to book her into the Regent — she particularly asked for the same hotel — and I'd like you to meet her at the airport. Jackie'll have the flight details for you."

I wanted to feel happy at the thought of seeing her again, but I'd fought to attain a fragile equilibrium, and I was fearful that she would not only destroy it, but by the time she left I'd be worse off than before.

Sir Frederick had been watching me. He said, "There's a difficulty?"

"Of course not," I said.

Lee's flight came in Friday morning. I hardly slept, and was early at the airport. I saw her before she saw me. Time telescoped: nothing had changed. She moved with self-assured, brisk impatience; I loved her with the same intensity.

In my imagination I'd rehearsed this meeting a hundred times and I had myself well-schooled in my role. I would protect myself, take my cues from her, be guided by her response.

She greeted me with a smile, but we didn't touch. I asked inconsequential questions about her flight while we walked to my car; she replied in kind. It was as though we had consulted and decided that we'd treat each other with cordial professional consideration and no reference would be made to anything personal.

As I drove her to the Regent we continued our light conversation. I was so keenly aware of her that I had to force myself to concentrate on the traffic, but I was confident she had no idea how I felt.

The stage lost a great actor, Alex, when you went into travel.

My sardonic thoughts were some protection — but not much. Why couldn't I say, casually, "Have you come back because you've found you can't live without me, after all?"

But that couldn't be true. There was nothing to indicate that anything had changed and Lee was probably here because of some hidden agenda that did not involve me.

As we arrived at the hotel, she said, "Tony told me about the fireworks with Sir Frederick."

I looked at her sharply. "Did he?"

Her smile was friendly, understanding. "From everything you've said before, I realize it's quite a step for you to take."

"It's something I had to do — and I feel fine about it."

She nodded. I wanted to say something more, to tell her that now I could understand the sense of freedom she'd spoken of in her own life, but she changed the subject.

"I'm going to freshen up and then come to the A.P.P. office. I've an appointment with Sir Frederick and then I'd like to see you to discuss the Tasmanian wilderness tours you faxed me details on."

I was looking at her hands and trying not to remember what she'd done to me with them. I nodded absently.

"Alex, I'd like to ask a favor."

That got my full attention. "Of course."

"Frankly, I need a break. Tomorrow's Saturday, and I wonder if it would be possible for us to do something — perhaps a cruise on the harbor ..."

"I've friends who've got a yacht. Trish and Suzie. They've already asked me to go sailing with them tomorrow, and I'm to ring them tonight to say if I can. Would you like to come too?"

Lee, decisive as ever, said, "Yes."

When I picked Lee up from her hotel on

Saturday morning the weather was gorgeous. The harbor was sparkling postcard blue, the sky innocent of anything but a few streaks of high cloud, the air warm, but with a breeze giving a slight bite to it.

We chatted, laughed, made trivial conversation as I drove across metallic splendor of the Sydney Harbour Bridge towards Mosman. Trish and Suzie's yacht was moored at Balmoral Beach, and we were to meet at the boatshed at ten o'clock.

During a moment when neither of us was trying to fill the silence, I glanced at her. She wore jeans, a plain white T-shirt and black canvas shoes. The strong lines of her face were achingly familiar and I could vividly remember the texture of her blonde hair, the planes of her back, the taut muscles under the smooth skin.

I can't bear it . . .

It was as though we had never made love, never known the intimate secrets of each other's bodies.

She was treating me as a dear friend, and I didn't dare question her on the depth of what she felt for me now — the potential for hurt was too great. I could cope with the situation as long as I kept playing my role. I knew exactly what to do — had a lifetime of practice — Lee's actions and reactions controlled my script. All I had to do was respond to cues. It was simple, safe and guaranteed to make life easier for everyone concerned.

By the time we arrived at the southern end of Balmoral Beach I had developed reservations about the weather. Trish and Suzie were waiting by their station wagon, a huge mound of essential sailing items — principally food and drink — at their feet.

I smiled at them affectionately. Trish has a soft

Canadian accent and silver-gray hair. Her brash good humor and irresponsible curiosity often lead her to ask comparative strangers astonishingly personal questions which for some reason most people answer willingly.

Suzie is more reserved, at least at first meeting. She reminds me of a sleek pedigreed cat — slim, contained and meditative.

Their reactions to Lee amused me. Trish, compulsively sociable, greeted her with the enthusiasm of a games show host. Suzie raised a speculative eyebrow, flashed me a look of approval, and gave Lee a warm "Hi."

The introductions over, I took the opportunity to voice my concern about the weather. "It looks like it might be a bit rough ..."

Suzie said, "You're such a sook, Alex!" Trish, more positively, assured me it was a perfect day for sailing. I felt the boisterous breeze against my face, looked at the little whitecaps it was creating, and doubted. Perhaps there's a seafaring gene missing in me. I delight in swimming in the ocean, admiring its scenic qualities, flying over its vastness, but I don't enjoy sailing on its surface when the water seems to have an obstreperous life of its own.

Lee obviously didn't share my doubts. She padded along the sagging planking that led to a dilapidated jetty, leaping with celerity into the battered metal dinghy that was to take us out to the *Water Nymph's* mooring. I was much more hesitant, because the surge of the sea made the boat buck alarmingly.

"Oh, go on!" said Suzie, never one to show patience with landlubbers.

173

I knew my friend well. "Don't push me, Suzie. If you push me I'm going home."

Lee extended a hand, Suzie timed the motion of the launch and, as I knew she would, gave me a firm shove at the appropriate moment. Trish ignored us all and kept feeding supplies to the boy who seemed far too youthful to be responsible for our lives. He stood with spread feet, holding the handle of the outboard motor with one hand, while grabbing each item from Trish when the boat came close enough. I admired his balance and timing, although he hadn't bothered to conceal his weary contempt of *my* marine abilities.

The *Water Nymph* is, in calmer seas, a beautiful little yacht. At a pinch she can sleep six, and she has a compact galley and dining area. She's white and sleek and good-humored and it's fun to sit in the stern — I'm never allowed to help with the sails — as we scud over the harbor. But when it's what Trish and Suzie call "good sailing weather" the vessel seems to gain a wicked, reckless life of her own, and, as she heels to the wind, I always get the uneasy feeling that she'd pitch me overboard if she had the chance.

I know my apprehensions make me endow the yacht with personality, but nevertheless this morning I detected a certain audacious, headstrong motion in *Water Nymph* when we'd motored out of the mooring area and the sails were set.

Trish and Suzie had tried to teach me the correct jargon, but apart from terms like port, starboard, forward and aft, my lack of commitment to sailing meant I referred to "that rope there," instead of the traditional "that sheet or that halyard." Lee, however, seemed to be perfectly familiar with everything, so she and Suzie worked the sails as we tacked, throwing esoteric yachting terms around as they obeyed Trish's peremptory commands from her position on the tiller. As usual, I pulled my cap down to shade my eyes and stayed out of the way.

I had to admit it was exhilarating running before the wind and Sydney Harbour was at its dazzling best. We avoided — narrowly, I thought — being run down by the Manly Jetcat ferry and tacked our way to a sheltered mooring off Forty Baskets Beach for lunch.

Trish and Suzie had made nautical lunch into an artform, and today, no doubt in honor of Lee, they'd done even better than usual. We lolled in the sun, sipped wine, buttered crusty bread and selected items from a plethora of little containers — sliced avocado, artichoke hearts, pâté, vine-leaf rolls, prawns, wedges of cheese, slices of prosciutto ...

Our conversation was light, full of laughter. Trish had a store of hilarious anecdotes from teaching, Suzie a similar collection from management. Lee seemed content to relax and be entertained. Once I looked up and caught her looking at me reflectively, but when I raised my eyebrows she just smiled.

All day she had been warm, responsive towards me, just as a close friend would be. There was nothing more.

This may be the best you can get ...

Listening to Lee's smoky laugh, I tried not to think of the past, or of the future.

In the afternoon we turned for home. To a landlubber like me, sailing seemed to consist of sudden flurries of activity, particularly when returning to a mooring. At this point I was always consigned to the cockpit, where I tried to keep out of the way of Trish on the tiller behind me, or Suzie leaping around on the top of the cabin bringing down the sails and then rushing forward with a boathook to pick up the mooring buoy as the yacht ran past it.

Today everything was progressing smoothly. Trish had started the motor, put it into gear, and was maneuvering skillfully between the moored vessels towards the yellow buoy marking their anchorage. Suzie and Lee had the mainsail down and were furling it on top of the boom.

The accident happened because of an insignificant piece of equipment — a little metal device with a lever to engage its set of metal teeth. Appropriately, it's called a rope jammer, because that's what it does.

One moment I was standing in the cockpit enjoying the bustle around me, the next moment the pain exploded in my head, a shattering burst of white light that faded to darkness. Then, confusingly, although I could see and feel nothing, I could hear, faintly, as though at a great distance, voices, one of them saying my name.

"Alex!"

Close by I heard a groan. When I realized the voice was mine, swamping, throbbing waves of pain filled my head.

Slowly I became aware of other things: my face pressed against something soft, my hip on a hard floor, arms holding me tightly.

"Alex, darling."

My eyes were squeezed tight against the pain,

but of greater importance was the knowledge of who held me, who said my name. It was Lee's heart thudding next to my cheek, Lee's arms holding me.

I tried to open my eyes, succeeded in letting a narrow crack of dazzling light speared into my brain, shut them again.

Lee's voice was a soft whisper against my cheek. "Alex. I know you're awake. Open your eyes."

I put a hand to my aching head, expecting warm blood, but there was nothing but my hair. I was on the floor of the cockpit, and so was Lee. She held me close against her, head bent over me, so that I could feel the brush of her breath on my face.

"I'm sorry I hurt you."

"What happened?"

"The boom fell on you," said Suzie helpfully.

Lee's arms tightened. "Alex, it was my fault."

I snuggled a little deeper into her breast. "Deliberate? You wanted to murder me?"

Trish sounded relieved. "If she's making jokes she's all right."

Suzie, who has a passion for detail, explained what had happened as we waited for the boat to pick us up from the mooring. "You were standing in the cockpit directly under the boom that supports the bottom of the mainsail. As Lee and I got the sail down and began to fold it along the boom, Lee accidentally kicked the rope jammer holding the topping lift. With it released, the boom dropped like a brick on top of your head. Simple."

Lee kept her arm around me, and when we reached the jetty she said, "I'm taking you to a doctor."

"I'm okay. I've just got a headache."

Lee said to Trish and Suzie, "You'll know the nearest medical center. I'll follow you in Alex's car."

I allowed myself to be put in the passenger seat of my own car, but I protested as Lee got behind the wheel. "Lee, we drive on the opposite side of the road to you."

"I'll be careful. Besides, this is an emergency — you might decide to sue me."

Even smiling made my head throb more. I shut my eyes. "The only way I'll sue you, Lee, is if you damage my car."

The doctor, a young Asian woman with gentle hands, had examined me and left me lying in the cubicle while she reported her findings to my little entourage.

They were on the other side of the flimsy partition and I could hear them talking. Suzie was saying, "So there's no fracture, just a slight concussion and someone has to keep an eye on her for twelve hours. Right, we'll take her home with us."

"No."

"Lee, we've got a spare room, and Trish and I can take it in turns to check she's all right."

"No. Alex's coming with me."

I opened my eyes. Raising my voice, I said, "I'll go with Lee . . . just to prevent an argument."

My car was nearby: Lee had parked in a *Medical Staff Only* area.

"Where are we going?" I asked as she turned the ignition key.

"To my hotel."

After a while, she said, "You know I didn't need to return to Australia. I used the tour as an excuse."

"Right."

"I had to come back to see you again."

I found I was holding my breath.

"Alex?"

"Yes."

"I needed to convince myself that I could live without you . . ."

When I didn't reply, she said wryly, "You have me at a disadvantage."

I jerked my head around to look at her, sending pain searing behind my eyes. "I have *you* at a disadvantage?"

"I don't know if you still love me, Alex. From the moment we met at the airport yesterday I realized that I want to be with you. But you've been so cool, so controlled : . ."

I closed my eyes. The uncertainty in her voice filled me with tenderness, and I smiled, but my voice showed only polite inquiry. "So I had to be knocked out before you'd be driven to say anything?"

Lee had been watching me. Her tone was suddenly warm, intimate. "No, darling. That just precipitated it. I was going to tell you tonight. I wasn't going to be able to wait any longer."

"You can't bring yourself to put it into words, can you Lee?"

"Sure I can. I love you, Alex." She waited until I opened my eyes. "Now it's your turn."

I couldn't stop smiling. "Oh, all right, if you insist. I love and adore you. I tried to stop and I couldn't. Satisfied?"

She nodded, took my hand, linking our fingers.

"Lee, are you sure you can drive with one hand on the wheel in a strange city on the wrong side of the road?"

"Of course," she said with all her old arrogance. Then, "I should warn you, Alex, this may not be love. I've only spent ninety-five percent of my time thinking about you for the past three months. You might want to wait for that missing five percent ..."

"That five percent's a worry," I said, "but, what the hell — I'll take the chance."

LOOKING FOR NAIAD?

SHATTERED ILLUSIONS by Kaye Davis. 256 pp. 4th
Maris Middleton mystery.   ISBN 1-56280-252-6   11.95

SET UP by Claire McNab. 224 pp. 11th Detective Inspector Carol
Ashton mystery.   ISBN 1-56280-255-0   11.95

THE DAWNING by Laura Adams. 224 pp. What if you had the
power to change the past?   ISBN 1-56280-246-1   11.95

NEVER ENDING by Marianne K. Martin. 224 pp. Temptation
appears in the form of an old friend and lover. ISBN 1-56280-247-X   11.95

ONE OF OUR OWN by Diane Salvatore. 240 pp. Carly Matson
has a secret. So does Lela Johns.   ISBN 1-56280-243-7   11.95

DOUBLE TAKEOUT by Tracey Richardson. 176 pp. 3rd Stevie
Houston mystery.   ISBN 1-56280-244-5   11.95

CAPTIVE HEART by Frankie J. Jones. 176 pp. Love in the
fast lane or heartside romance?   ISBN 1-56280-258-5   11.95

WICKED GOOD TIME by Diana Tremain Braund. 224 pp. In
charge at work, out of control in her heart. ISBN 1-56280-241-0   11.95

SNAKE EYES by Pat Welch. 256 pp. 7th Helen Black mystery.
                                             ISBN 1-56280-242-9   11.95

CHANGE OF HEART by Linda Hill. 176 pp. High fashion and
love in a glamorous world.   ISBN 1-56280-238-0   11.95

UNSTRUNG HEART by Robbi Sommers. 176 pp. Putting life
in order again.   ISBN 1-56280-239-9   11.95

BIRDS OF A FEATHER by Jackie Calhoun. 240 pp. Life begins
with love.   ISBN 1-56280-240-2   11.95

THE DRIVE by Trisha Todd. 176 pp. The star of *Claire of the
Moon* tells all!   ISBN 1-56280-237-2   11.95

BOTH SIDES by Saxon Bennett. 240 pp. A community of
women falling in and out of love.   ISBN 1-56280-236-4   11.95

WATERMARK by Karin Kallmaker. 256 pp. One burning
question . . . how to lead her back to love? ISBN 1-56280-235-6   11.95

THE OTHER WOMAN by Ann O'Leary. 240 pp. Her roguish
way draws women like a magnet.   ISBN 1-56280-234-8   11.95

SILVER THREADS by Lyn Denison.208 pp. Finding her way
back to love . . .   ISBN 1-56280-231-3   11.95

CHIMNEY ROCK BLUES by Janet McClellan. 224 pp. 4th Tru
North mystery.   ISBN 1-56280-233-X   11.95

OMAHA'S BELL by Penny Hayes. 208 pp. Orphaned Keeley
Delaney woos the lovely Prudence Morris.   ISBN 1-56280-232-1   11.95

SIXTH SENSE by Kate Calloway. 224 pp. 6th Cassidy James
mystery.   ISBN 1-56280-228-3   11.95

DAWN OF THE DANCE by Marianne K. Martin. 224 pp. A dance
with an old friend, nothing more . . . yeah! ISBN 1-56280-229-1   11.95

THOSE WHO WAIT by Peggy J. Herring. 160 pp. Two
sisters . . . in love with the same woman.   ISBN 1-56280-223-2   11.95

WHISPERS IN THE WIND by Frankie J. Jones. 192 pp. "If you
don't want this," she whispered, "all you have to say is 'stop.' "
ISBN 1-56280-226-7   11.95

WHEN SOME BODY DISAPPEARS by Therese Szymanski.
192 pp. 3rd Brett Higgins mystery.   ISBN 1-56280-227-5   11.95

UNTIL THE END by Kaye Davis. 256pp. 3rd Maris Middleton
mystery.   ISBN 1-56280-222-4   11.95

FIFTH WHEEL by Kate Calloway. 224 pp. 5th Cassidy James
mystery.   ISBN 1-56280-218-6   11.95

JUST YESTERDAY by Linda Hill. 176 pp. Reliving all the
passion of yesterday.   ISBN 1-56280-219-4   11.95

THE TOUCH OF YOUR HAND edited by Barbara Grier and
Christine Cassidy. 304 pp. Erotic love stories by Naiad Press
authors.   ISBN 1-56280-220-8   14.95

PAST DUE by Claire McNab. 224 pp. 10th Carol Ashton
mystery.   ISBN 1-56280-217-8   11.95

CHRISTABEL by Laura Adams. 224 pp. Two captive hearts and
the passion that will set them free.   ISBN 1-56280-214-3   11.95

PRIVATE PASSIONS by Laura DeHart Young. 192 pp. An
unforgettable new portrait of lesbian love . . .   ISBN 1-56280-215-1   11.95

BAD MOON RISING by Barbara Johnson. 208 pp. 2nd Colleen
Fitzgerald mystery.   ISBN 1-56280-211-9   11.95

RIVER QUAY by Janet McClellan. 208 pp. 3rd Tru North
mystery.   ISBN 1-56280-212-7   11.95

ENDLESS LOVE by Lisa Shapiro. 272 pp. To believe, once
again, that love can be forever.   ISBN 1-56280-213-5   11.95

FALLEN FROM GRACE by Pat Welch. 256 pp. 6th Helen Black
mystery.   ISBN 1-56280-209-7   11.95

OVER THE LINE by Tracey Richardson. 176 pp. 2nd Stevie
Houston mystery.   ISBN 1-56280-202-X   11.95

LOVE IN THE BALANCE by Marianne K. Martin. 256 pp.
Weighing the costs of love . . .   ISBN 1-56280-199-6   11.95

PIECE OF MY HEART by Julia Watts. 208 pp. All the
stuff that dreams are made of —   ISBN 1-56280-206-2   11.95

MAKING UP FOR LOST TIME by Karin Kallmaker. 240 pp.
Nobody does it better . . .   ISBN 1-56280-196-1   11.95

GOLD FEVER by Lyn Denison. 224 pp. By author of *Dream
Lover*.   ISBN 1-56280-201-1   11.95

WHEN THE DEAD SPEAK by Therese Szymanski. 224 pp. 2nd
Brett Higgins mystery.   ISBN 1-56280-198-8   11.95

FOURTH DOWN by Kate Calloway. 240 pp. 4th Cassidy James
mystery.   ISBN 1-56280-193-7   11.95

CITY LIGHTS COUNTRY CANDLES by Penny Hayes. 208 pp.
About the women she has known . . .   ISBN 1-56280-195-3   11.95

POSSESSIONS by Kaye Davis. 240 pp. 2nd Maris Middleton
mystery.   ISBN 1-56280-192-9   11.95

A QUESTION OF LOVE by Saxon Bennett. 208 pp. Every
woman is granted one great love.   ISBN 1-56280-205-4   11.95

RHYTHM TIDE by Frankie J. Jones. 160 pp.   . . . to desire
passionately and be passionately desired.   ISBN 1-56280-189-9   11.95

PENN VALLEY PHOENIX by Janet McClellan. 208 pp. 2nd
Tru North Mystery.   ISBN 1-56280-200-3   11.95

OLD BLACK MAGIC by Jaye Maiman. 272 pp. 6th Robin
Miller mystery.   ISBN 1-56280-175-9   11.95

LETTING GO by Ann O'Leary. 160 pp. Laura, at 39, in love
with 23-year-old Kate.   ISBN 1-56280-183-X   11.95

LADY BE GOOD edited by Barbara Grier and Christine Cassidy.
288 pp. Erotic stories by Naiad Press authors.   ISBN 1-56280-180-5   14.95

CHAIN LETTER by Claire McNab. 288 pp. 9th Carol Ashton
mystery.   ISBN 1-56280-181-3   11.95

NIGHT VISION by Laura Adams. 256 pp. Erotic fantasy romance
by "famous" author.   ISBN 1-56280-182-1   11.95

SEA TO SHINING SEA by Lisa Shapiro. 256 pp. Unable to resist
the raging passion . . .   ISBN 1-56280-177-5   11.95

THIRD DEGREE by Kate Calloway. 224 pp. 3rd Cassidy James
mystery.   ISBN 1-56280-185-6   11.95

WHEN THE DANCING STOPS by Therese Szymanski. 272 pp.
1st Brett Higgins mystery.   ISBN 1-56280-186-4   11.95

PHASES OF THE MOON by Julia Watts. 192 pp. . . . . hungry
for everything life has to offer.   ISBN 1-56280-176-7   11.95

BABY IT'S COLD by Jaye Maiman. 256 pp. 5th Robin Miller
mystery.   ISBN 1-56280-156-2   10.95

CLASS REUNION by Linda Hill. 176 pp. The girl from her
past . . .   ISBN 1-56280-178-3   11.95

FORTY LOVE by Diana Simmonds. 288 pp. Joyous, heart-
warming romance.   ISBN 1-56280-171-6   11.95

IN THE MOOD by Robbi Sommers. 160 pp. The queen of
erotic tension!   ISBN 1-56280-172-4   11.95

SWIMMING CAT COVE by Lauren Wright Douglas. 192 pp. 2nd
Allison O'Neil Mystery.   ISBN 1-56280-168-6   11.95

THE LOVING LESBIAN by Claire McNab and Sharon Gedan.
240 pp. Explore the experiences that make lesbian love unique.
ISBN 1-56280-169-4   14.95

COURTED by Celia Cohen. 160 pp. Sparkling romantic
encounter.   ISBN 1-56280-166-X   11.95

SEASONS OF THE HEART by Jackie Calhoun. 240 pp. Romance
through the years.   ISBN 1-56280-167-8   11.95

K. C. BOMBER by Janet McClellan. 208 pp. 1st Tru North
mystery.   ISBN 1-56280-157-0   11.95

LAST RITES by Tracey Richardson. 192 pp. 1st Stevie Houston
mystery.   ISBN 1-56280-164-3   11.95

EMBRACE IN MOTION by Karin Kallmaker. 256 pp. A whirlwind
love affair.   ISBN 1-56280-165-1   11.95

HOT CHECK by Peggy J. Herring. 192 pp. Will workaholic Alice
fall for guitarist Ricky?   ISBN 1-56280-163-5   11.95

OLD TIES by Saxon Bennett. 176 pp. Can Cleo surrender to a
passionate new love?   ISBN 1-56280-159-7   11.95

COSTA BRAVA by Marta Balletbo-Coll. 144 pp. Read the book,
see the movie!   ISBN 1-56280-160-0   11.95

MEETING MAGDALENE & OTHER STORIES by
Marilyn Freeman. 144 pp. Read the book, see the movie!
ISBN 1-56280-170-8   11.95

SECOND FIDDLE by Kate Kalloway. 208 pp. 2nd P.I. Cassidy James
mystery.   ISBN 1-56280-161-9   11.95

LAUREL by Isabel Miller. 128 pp. By the author of the beloved
Patience and Sarah.   ISBN 1-56280-146-5   10.95

LOVE OR MONEY by Jackie Calhoun. 240 pp. The romance of
real life.   ISBN 1-56280-147-3   10.95

SMOKE AND MIRRORS by Pat Welch. 224 pp. 5th Helen Black
Mystery.   ISBN 1-56280-143-0   10.95

DANCING IN THE DARK edited by Barbara Grier & Christine
Cassidy. 272 pp. Erotic love stories by Naiad Press authors.
ISBN 1-56280-144-9   14.95

TIME AND TIME AGAIN by Catherine Ennis. 176 pp. Passionate
love affair.   ISBN 1-56280-145-7   10.95

These are just a few of the many Naiad Press titles — we are the oldest and
largest lesbian/feminist publishing company in the world. We also offer an
enormous selection of lesbian video products. Please request a complete
catalog. We offer personal service; we encourage and welcome direct mail
orders from individuals who have limited access to bookstores carrying our
publications.